A
Mistake

A
Mistake

A Novel

Carl Shuker

COUNTERPOINT
Berkeley, California

A Mistake

Library of Congress Cataloging-in-Publication Data
Names: Shuker, R. Carl, 1974– author.
Title: A mistake / Carl Shuker.
Description: First Counterpoint hardcover edition. | Berkeley, California :
Counterpoint, 2019.
Identifiers: LCCN 2019004433 | ISBN 9781640092495
Classification: LCC PR9639.4.S56 M57 2019 | DDC 823/.92—dc23
LC record available at https://lccn.loc.gov/2019004433

Jacket design by Sarah Brody

COUNTERPOINT
2560 Ninth Street, Suite 318
Berkeley, CA 94710
www.counterpointpress.com

Printed in the United States of America
Distributed by Publishers Group West

1 3 5 7 9 10 8 6 4 2

For Carl James Patton

Flight controllers here are looking very carefully at the situation. Obviously a major malfunction.

—Space Shuttle *Challenger* launch commentary

A
Mistake

A glass of milk with Voltaren and Panadeine

'Hello there,' Elizabeth said, leaning over the girl, smiling. 'Hello. Hello Lisa.' The girl looked up at her accusingly. 'My name is Elizabeth Taylor. Please call me Liz. I'm the consultant surgeon and this is my registrar, Richard Whitehead.'

Elizabeth smiled wider for her.

'How are you feeling?'

The girl lay in the bed in the emergency department and she was pale and very sick and there were black bruises under her eyes. She had an IV in one arm and was in her very early twenties. A white girl, small and thin and turning in her pillows, selfish, inward in her pain.

She looked away to the ED nurse who had been waiting with her. The nurse was a middle-aged Englishman standing with his feet together. He had a tag on his chest that read

#HelloMyNameIs
Awesome

with *Awesome* crossed out and *Matt* written underneath in Biro.

'Where's the doctor—' the girl said.

Richard was beside Elizabeth, turning through the notes and murmuring.

'She's tachycardic,' he said. 'Up from an hour ago. Respiration 22 and steady, pressure is down, is why we paged.'

The girl looked past Elizabeth to the male nurse, and she said, 'My shoulder. My shoulder hurts.'

Matt leaned down to her and he said, kindly, 'Does it hurt in your shoulder now?'

'Yes.'

'Does it hurt when you breathe?' said Elizabeth.

The girl looked at her wide-eyed and she said yes, and turned to Matt again and Matt watched her eyes, half-smiling down at her.

'Okay. That's okay,' he said.

'She's got no pain at McBurney's point,' Richard said. 'Doesn't look like appendix. She's had a total of 10 milligrams of morphine since 9:30 for increasing pain and 10 milligrams of Maxolon for the nausea.'

'Where are you from Lisa?' said Elizabeth in a conversational voice. 'Lisa? Where do you live?'

'Rotorua,' the girl said, like a question.

'Are you on holiday in Wellington?' said Elizabeth. 'We're having a lovely summer down here aren't we. Get out of the way,' and Matt stepped quickly sideways.

Elizabeth pulled the gown off the girl's stomach. She pressed gently on the right side above her appendix. The girl squinted and tensed. Then Elizabeth pressed gently on the left side of her stomach by a cluster of small moles and the girl half-squealed in a low wheezing exhalation. Her eyes outraged and wet.

'Did that hurt, Lisa?' said Elizabeth. 'I'm sorry. You be brave now.'

The girl had started to cry and was looking at Matt. She made a keening sound then she said, 'Where's the *other* doctor?'

'GP at Adelaide Road saw her three days ago,' Richard said to the notes. 'One day of cramping abdominal pain. Soft and tender abdomen with guarding at left iliac. Given trimethoprim, diclofenac, paracetamol, and sent away. She came back again three days later, from some camping ground in the Hutt, in a lot of pain. No bowel motion or urine for two days, elevated pulse, and they put her on IV fluids and transferred her here. Radiology suggests necrosis to bowel and organs and notes there's an IUCD in situ.'

Elizabeth listened and looked down kindly at the girl.

'Lisa,' said Elizabeth. 'Lisa. Are you pregnant, Lisa?'

'No. No, I don't think so. No? Is it a baby? Is it a *baby*?' she said and she stared at Elizabeth and at Matt.

Richard flicked through the notes.

'BhCG negative. It was added to the labs.'

'Who did that,' murmured Elizabeth.

'It was a locum I think,' said Richard and looked around the ED.

'Good for them,' said Elizabeth. 'Someone's on the ball. Who's with her? Do you have someone with you like a boyfriend or your parents, Lisa?'

The girl looked left and right. Her breathing becoming more shallow, more desperate.

'The boyfriend's outside,' said Matt.

'Is your boyfriend with you Lisa?' said Elizabeth. 'What's your boyfriend's name? Is he from Rotorua too?'

The girl looked left and right again. 'Stuart,' she said and as she spoke Elizabeth pushed her stomach down again above her left hipbone with three fingers and this time the girl screamed.

'Okay now, we're going to take care of you, Lisa,' Elizabeth said. 'You be brave now.'

5

'Where's the *doctor*,' she said, very angry now, and Elizabeth ignored her.

'Well,' she said to Richard.

'Uh,' he said, and he looked at the chart. 'Clearly . . . intra-abdominal catastrophe. Immediate surgery to assess for ruptured viscus, bowel or appendix. Aggressive fluids and transfer to theatre for laparoscopy.'

Elizabeth said, 'Well. Possibly. I think we'd rather provisionally suggest pelvic peritonitis maybe due to salpingitis. You said yourself she had no pain at McBurney's and this was confirmed by examination right in front of you. Why add appendix to that list? Leaving yourself outs? I agree with the immediate urgent laparoscopy. Three units of packed red blood cells crossmatched and prep for theatre and page Dr Mirnov to consent her.'

Richard was nodding and nodding and staring at the notes.

Elizabeth turned back to the girl.

She was moaning and had closed her eyes.

In the corridors from ED to theatre Elizabeth's sneakers slapped and squeaked. Her father's only daughter, 42 years old, youngest and the only woman consultant general surgeon at Wellington. Sudden bursts of light as the sun went west over the valley as she walked and her sneakers slapped and squeaked on the shining linoleum. Mid-afternoon, now, clouds creeping south over Newtown. There was a black-eyed little sparrow trapped inside the hospital, testing the windows, flying from sill to sill down the corridor. As she walked she called Simon Martin to get on with a boring hernia repair she'd been about to begin when she was paged and then she called theatre to get ready for this girl.

'Robin,' she said into the phone. 'Prep for laparoscopy and a peritoneal washout and removal of IUCD. She's septic and will need antibiotic cover. Tell Vladimir we're on our way. How *are* you, anyway?'

Elizabeth's voice was cheery and pleasant. She had been up for 27 hours. This was the end of her on-call. She was so constipated she had not used the toilet in two days. It was useful for operating. She hadn't drunk any liquids but coffee all day and her bowels burned and felt dry and heavy and wooden, reliable.

As she walked through the interrupted glares of southern sun Elizabeth had an abrupt verbatim recall of a brutal peer review comment she had received yesterday. It was a revise and resubmit on an editorial she and Andrew had sent to the *Royal London Journal of Medicine*, about the upcoming public reporting of surgical outcomes in New Zealand.

These authors have conflated several very different, very important issues and failed to produce a meaningful interpretation that usefully advances our understanding of any of them.

Andrew McGrath was head of surgery and dean of the Wellington campus of the Otago Medical School. It was her job to reply to the journal on their behalf. The *Royal London Journal of Medicine* was one of the Big Three, alongside *The Lancet* and the *BMJ*, most prestigious medical journals in the UK. Impact factor: intimidating. The third oldest medical journal in the world. Even to be gutted at peer review was something of a coup. Andrew would be in the corridors. Andrew would be at the upcoming conference in Queenstown.

She'd better have something ready.

Elizabeth bore down, she focused, and the solution came, as it always did for her, when she bore down.

'Robin, please make a note for me,' she said as she walked. 'Say: we are grateful for this reviewer's comment and upon reflection we have adjusted those paragraphs at lines 120–130. I'll recheck that. Say: however, we regret we cannot agree with his view given his previously published partisan position on public reporting of surgeons' outcomes in the *Royal London*—2013 I think it was, I'll check that, Robin—and something something really vicious there, and delete those paragraphs and replace with a reference to Carnaby et al., 2012, that's C-A-R-N-A-B-Y, and say this quote: "For a successful technology, reality must take precedence over public relations, for nature cannot be fooled." That's Richard P. Feynman who said that. F-E-Y-N-M-A-N.'

She saw herself moving in reflection in the hospital windows as the sun hit her. Small, straight-backed and uniformed in blue scrubs. Happy. The bird bumping against the glass inside her. Would it die in here?

Go, she said to herself, and disappeared again in the shadow.

'I'll check it but it's something very close to that, anyway. All good?'

Robin was speaking.

'Hold on.'

She flicked through the notes as she walked.

'Yep. Last oral intake 7:30 this morning. She had a glass of milk, Voltaren and Panadeine.'

The girl was asleep. Her belly button all that was visible in the centre of a square of pale skin formed by the blue drapes. At her shoulders the drapes became a great blue crucifix shielding her head and Vladimir, sitting on his stool by the anaesthetic machine.

Elizabeth, gloved and gowned, said, 'Now.'

Everyone, even the circulating nurse, stopped moving.

'We will perform a classic Hasson open technique. Why?'

The nurses came back to life and moved about the theatre. Elizabeth pinched a fold of fat on the girl's stomach with gloved fingers and squeezed it to open up her belly button. Richard leaned forward and widened the navel with the Littlewoods forceps.

'Let's give it a clean first, Richard,' she said.

'Sorry.'

'Inevitably you will encounter material in the umbilicus initial prep has missed.'

The comment was directed at Josie the scrub nurse and she looked up.

'It's clean,' Josie said.

'We'll see,' Elizabeth said.

'Do you want to do the checklist, Doctor?' said Mei-Lynn. She was indicating the large poster of the surgical safety checklist on the theatre wall.

'No, we don't have time. Let's get on with it. Now'—the doors flapped behind her as Richard scrubbed the girl's belly button with a swab in forceps—'get in there. Clean it properly.'

The doors flapped closed. The nurses had parted. Someone new was there. Elizabeth leaned back, rolled her neck in her shoulders and leaned down again to the belly button.

'Hello, Andrew,' she said.

'Hello, everyone,' he said. He was behind her, not scrubbed, wearing his double-breasted suit. 'Carry on. Just looking in.'

'For the benefit of those new here, Andrew McGrath, head of surgery. Welcome, Andrew.'

'Yes, yes,' he said. 'Carry on.'

Elizabeth met eyes with Robin across the girl's stomach. Elizabeth grinned at her but Robin didn't let her eyes change.

'Now. Why Hasson.'

Richard glanced up at Andrew as he cleaned and back down again. 'Um, a 2014 review,' Richard said, 'found major and minor complications a percentage point safer for, um, open technique versus the Veress needle?'

'But that particular study was an Indian review,' said Elizabeth. She stood over the patient, pinching the girl's stomach. 'Context matters. Number five blade please.'

Andrew moved closer to the edge of the sterile field, almost standing among them to get a better view.

'Andrew and I,' Elizabeth said, 'are working on a paper about publishing our outcomes. For a medical journal you might just have heard of called the *Royal London Journal of Medicine*. Aren't we Andrew? Bit controversial. Publishing our numbers in the papers. Complications and patient deaths of named surgeons. Which for one we think ignores the stellar contribution to this girl's care made by all of you.'

'Mmm,' Andrew said. 'Well, quite.'

He leaned forward to watch.

Elizabeth took the scalpel from Robin and punctured the skin beneath the girl's belly button and in one bloodless cut incised straight down a single centimetre.

She said, 'And we've had a peer review come back that's been let's say somewhat suspicious of our conclusions.'

A couple of the nurses sniffed soft laughter. Richard flicked his eyes up to Andrew and back down again.

'That peer review,' Andrew said, 'is from an Oxford don who's actually Australian. He's very partisan on the issue of publishing outcomes. And he doesn't like me.'

The nurses looked at nothing but the operation and the instruments.

'I've got a few ideas,' Elizabeth said.

'Very good,' he said.

'First of all—'

'We can discuss it later,' he said.

She stared at the incision. She felt her left eye twitch. She was tired. She made herself not look at Richard, or Robin. That sudden rage; it was interesting. She made herself find it interesting. She held it and turned it and examined it. How susceptible she was to the hand that pats the head not patting. And she used it to focus.

She placed the scalpel back on the tray and took the forceps and reached inside the wound and grasped a piece of the tough tissue under the belly button and pulled it up through the hole she had made. Richard grasped it with forceps on the other side and she took up the scalpel again and sliced a line down through it. Robin reached in with her forceps and grasped another piece of the tissue and they pulled it up and Elizabeth steadily cut her way through the stiff fascia, faster than she normally might. It was wet and white even against the girl's pale skin but there was no blood. A little white bud of meat protruding at her belly button.

'Just a few fibres at a time,' Elizabeth said. Then, as she sliced, 'The Cochrane review covered 46 randomised controlled trials of 13 laparoscopic techniques. What did they find, Richard?'

Richard said, 'Um, they found with Hasson technique no events in any of 12,000 patient days, I think it was 12,000 wasn't it, it was a lot, for mortality, gas embolism, or internal injury.'

'It also found Veress needle method will score lower every time,' she said. 'Failed entry, vascular injury, visceral injury. Veress loses every time and if you assist a surgeon who attempts it you're endangering the patient. It's bullshit. Bad medicine. Now we see the peritoneum.'

The peritoneum was visible. Inside the small hole: a taut, veined white bag. Elizabeth pinched the fat fold and lifted it, pulling at the stomach. 'We give it some traction,' she murmured, 'why.'

'To avoid uh, to avoid damaging the underlying structures when we um, penetrate the peritoneal sheath into the abdomen.'

'Yep, Richard.'

She leaned down with her forceps. The small hole was now held open with three pairs of forceps grasping tissue, and pressure from her pinch. She pushed the forceps into the hole and pushed it against the peritoneum until it popped through into the girl's abdominal cavity. Behind her Andrew moved slightly to get a better view. She opened the forceps like scissors to widen the opening and then removed them and pushed her whole finger inside the hole in the girl's belly and felt around inside for adhesions, for rips in the hole. When she removed her finger Robin leaned down and pushed a wide smooth retractor like a shoehorn inside the hole. The girl's belly joggled and shifted and a clear fluid tinged with yellow was filling the hole but Robin held the retractor steady as Elizabeth leaned her forceps into it for leverage to sew a purse-string stitch, left and right. It was like a dance, but there was less pleasure in it now, being good, because it was a performance before him.

Elizabeth picked up the trocar from the tray. This one had

12

no blade. It was a short blue pipe with taps around a handle like a thick screwdriver and she took the retractor from Robin and used the retractor like a plank to ease the pipe into the hole in the girl's belly on a diagonal, screwing it left and right, drawing the leaking fluid to help it in.

'Hasson,' she said as she screwed it in, 'has a small incision which leaves little or no scarring enhancing postoperative recovery. Hasson allows access under vision. Hasson won't puncture the bowel.'

'Thank you all,' said Andrew. 'Carry on.'

'Thanks, Andrew,' she said. 'Get what you needed?'

'Just checking in,' he said.

'Checking in.'

'Yes.'

'Cheers, then,' she said.

'Yes, yes,' he said.

'Cheers, cheers,' Elizabeth said and grinned at Robin and the doors flapped closed.

There was a momentary pause and she blinked and breathed out through her nose.

'Right,' she said. 'Let's get on with helping this girl. We will be inserting three trocars into Lisa today. Trocar, from the French *trois*, meaning three and *carre*, or edge. The three edges of the blade opening a portal into the abdomen into which we now have access—12-millimetre for camera, light and gas to blow up her abdomen thus creating a pneumoperitoneum for us to work within, and 5- and 8-millimetre for other instruments as needed, and for drainage. We're inserting three ports today, including camera, at the risk of repeating myself. Now. Maestro?'

They were smiling behind their masks as she made her small speech.

'Yes?' said Mei-Lynn.

'Can you for crying out loud put the Slayer on, please. The 30-minute one.'

Robin audibly exhaled.

'No,' someone breathed.

'Oh, come on,' said Vladimir from behind the anaesthetic machine.

'Do it,' she said, and laughed at them. 'Did you know, Richard, a recent study out of the US showed women physicians have measurably better outcomes than the men? *Journal of the American Medical Association* this year. Huge sample size too. Something to think about for all of us. And our dear leaders.' The nurses were smiling and the atmosphere had changed again. 'Did you also know,' she said, leaning down, 'first recorded use of the trocar was in 30 AD? Aulus Cornelius Celsus in the *De Medicina*. Originally used to drain fluids and gas from the abdomen. And that, my dears, is more or less what we'll be doing today, 2000 years on.'

The two surgeons stood across from each other, their hands raised as if blessing the girl's body before them, frozen for a moment. Robin screwed the gas pipe to the side of the trocar in the girl's belly.

'Gas, please,' said Elizabeth.

The music began. Slayer's *Angel of Death*, a thrash metal song that had been remixed until it was 30 minutes long. She liked to play it on repeat. It was hypnotic and repetitive and it helped her concentrate. The single metal riff that opened the song repeated and repeated and a German voice murmured above it. The girl's abdomen rose as the gas inflated it like a pregnancy.

'That's the stuff,' whispered Elizabeth, to the music, and to the pneumoperitoneum.

Robin took up the pipe of the camera and slid it into the end of the trocar and inside the girl's body.

Above them on the screens shifting veils of flesh emerged from darkness.

'Well, look at that,' Elizabeth said. On the screen the tissues were red and inflamed. There were brown pits of abscesses along her fallopian tubes.

'Extensive pus,' Richard said.

'Yep. Second trocar, please,' Elizabeth said.

She made a small press cut at the lower left of the girl's belly with her scalpel and took up the second smaller trocar.

'Left lower quadrant, direct vision please, Richard,' she said and he rotated the camera. 'We insert the trocar under direct vision to ensure no damage to the underlying structures,' she said. She pushed the trocar against the cut and the skin dimpled gently. The trocar's sleeve, its blade extending at the pressure, cut and sank into the girl. Above them on screen the blue plastic tube emerged huge into the frame inside her, and the blade vanished away.

Then the girl's abdomen sank slightly. The song's riff repeated and repeated and the German voice murmured on.

'Can we check gas flow please, Mei-Lynn,' Elizabeth said.

Mei-Lynn went to the gas tower.

'Extensive pus, indicating what do you think, Richard?' Elizabeth said up to the screens. She pressed with her fingers on the girl's tummy. Then to Mei-Lynn—'I want ten mercury. What's wrong with the gas? Richard, do you want to insert the last port?'

'Yep, sure.'

Richard took up the last trocar from the tray like a dagger, the wrong way around, then inverted it so it rose from his fist.

He looked up and saw she was watching.

'How's that pressure please,' Elizabeth said, looking at him. 'Extensive pus, indicating—?'

Mei-Lynn was at the tower and said, 'Um, pressure is set to ten and flow rate is six but we're not at ten yet.'

'Have you changed the gas for Christ's sake,' Elizabeth said to the screen. 'Go and get a new bottle.'

The Slayer droned on and on and it was very quiet otherwise after Mei-Lynn had left the room.

Robin went to the tower.

Richard hovered for a moment above the pale skin and Elizabeth looked down from the screen at him.

'What's up, Doctor?'

'No problem—'

Elizabeth touched the skin in the very corner of the visible square of her stomach. 'Is that the 5-millimetre?'

'Uh—' He checked it. 'Yes.'

'Well let's get on with it. What's wrong with that gas, Robin?'

Robin said, 'The bottle's full.'

'Well, increase the flow. Come on.'

Richard took up a scalpel and made a small incision at the top right of her abdomen where she'd touched the skin and put the scalpel back down again. He placed the tip of the trocar against the small slit.

Robin pressed a button on the tower. 'That's six point five,' she said and they watched the abdomen rise again.

'Come on then,' Elizabeth said. 'This young woman is very sick and may be dying in front of us.'

Richard pushed the trocar hard into the girl and it sank slightly and stopped.

Elizabeth stared up at the screen with the camera handle

in one hand. 'You're not through,' she said. 'Hurry up. Give it some welly. Indicating what, Richard?'

'Indicating—' he said, and he pushed the trocar into the girl.

On screen sudden bright blood rose in the seams of the red geography of the inflamed tissues. They watched as the blood filled the cavity. It rose and it rose and it did not stop, and so close on the tiny camera, lapping gently as if in a breeze.

'—cut the mesenteric,' Elizabeth said normally. She stepped back from the girl on the bed and raised her hands before her chest. Normally, she said, 'Quick, we have to open.'

The Slayer was now playing the first riff with drums. Every change was elaborated at length because it was a remix of a three-minute song into a version 30 minutes long. The blood was filling her abdomen completely. Richard stood and looked at the screen. Like its meaning defeated him. Every change went forever until it collapsed into noise and resolved into the new change and everyone knew it was an Elizabeth Taylor favourite. The nurses were stopped and they were looking around.

Robin said, '—are we converting?'

'Can someone please call fucking Mei-Lynn back in here?' Elizabeth said normally. 'How's she doing, anaesthesia?'

'Uh,' Vladimir said, 'systolic 90. Pressure is falling now.'

'Robin, remove all the laparoscopic gear. B tray for urgent laparotomy and arterial instruments. Music off, get all this gear out of the way now.'

Robin stepped forward and grasped the camera handle. On the screen above them the image of the curved organs and the abdominal wall and the pools and bubbles of dark blood they lay within lapped and wobbled and then shot away, it all collapsed upon itself and disappeared down a tube and flew about the room, capturing their masked faces in single blurred frames as Robin pulled the camera from the port and dumped the apparatus on a trolley. She pulled the ports and trocars from the girl's abdomen one by one, reaching in front of Richard to take the last one out, the hollow dagger that had stabbed the sleeping girl inside.

Mei-Lynn came back into the OR carrying the CO_2 cylinder hanging heavy from one hand. She stopped when she saw the two surgeons motionless and Robin piling the tubes and instruments on the trolley.

Mei-Lynn looked around her. Then she leaned the CO_2 cylinder down against the wall and came forward.

Robin hissed, 'B tray quick, we're opening.'

Elizabeth said, 'Hurry up you silly cunt.'

Mei-Lynn turned and went quickly back out for the instruments.

The CO_2 cylinder she'd left behind her slid slow then fast down the wall. It hit the ground and bounced and rolled away under the trolleys with brassy thunder.

'Christ,' said Elizabeth.

Before them the visible square of the girl's stomach was still. The small holes bloodless and waiting and under them the chaos gathered.

Josie came forward to adjust the drapes.

'Get out of it,' said Elizabeth, and she stepped back again. 'Robin. The B tray and the arterial instruments. How long will we have to wait.'

Robin came forward with a fresh trolley and adjusted the drapes.

'Vladi?' said Elizabeth.

'Pressure is still falling. She is becoming difficult to ventilate.'

Elizabeth stared up at the clock.

'I called for three units of red blood cells pre-op, can you please ask Betty to get the blood.'

'Yes Doctor.'

'Where are the fucking instruments please.'

Robin turned to the doors but Mei-Lynn had returned with the tray and laid it out, peeling back the sterile parcels. Elizabeth reached out and pushed them aside and took up the scalpel. In one stroke she made a foot-long cut the length of the girl's belly between the leaking hole at her belly button and the hole for the port above her left hip. The skin dropped open and dark blood rose in spots in the white fat.

'Diathermy,' Robin said to Mei-Lynn.

'No, we don't have time,' Elizabeth said. 'I'll do it myself.'

Around her the theatre staff stopped to watch what she was going to do. Elizabeth placed her gloved index finger against the side of the blade to control the depth of the incision and sliced in one long cut down again through the subcutaneous fat and sheaths of muscle and the peritoneum all at once and the girl's bowel opened up and it was full of bright dark blood and the blood shone and moved freely about the organs so their colours and shapes were indistinguishable.

'Vladi,' Elizabeth said calmly.

'Heart rate is 140.'

She leaned in and began to separate and divide the small intestines with her hands. Richard had not moved since he had inserted the trocar. Robin placed the suction tube at the side of the wound and the blood sank quickly. The only sound in the room was its sound, the gurgling inhalation and the grind of the machine. Elizabeth used both hands to lift and separate the heavy organs. She lifted them and looked and replaced them and moved them to one side.

'There,' she said. 'There. And there. Suction. Put your finger on it.' Robin reached in. 'Not you,' Elizabeth said. 'Richard. You cut her.'

Robin swabbed the cavity with a piece of gauze and for a moment they saw the small dark slit in the back of the abdominal wall pumping blood. Richard pressed his finger against it before it disappeared. Their white gloves were up to their wrists in red. Elizabeth moved on and lifted the loops of small intestine, the slab of liver, the inflamed uterus, parting the organs, pushing the sick fallopians aside as the well filled with blood again.

'There. There's a cut in the IVC here and we need to extend the incision to clamp it,' Elizabeth said.

She took up the scalpel again and extended the opening in the girl's belly high and low in small tugging cuts. Robin added another retractor to pull back the skin and fascia of her stomach then leaned in. Elizabeth teased up the thick, leaking vein and held it with one finger over the cut. Robin clamped it above and below with steel clamps then suctioned out the blood and reached in to mop up with a wad of gauze and yet more bright blood filled the seams. There were five hands and four clamps inside the girl's abdomen.

'Careful with the ureter. Stay where you are. *Govern these ventages with your fingers and thumb,*' she murmured, and sniffed a soft laugh.

She lifted her finger from the rent in the vena cava and it did not bleed any more. They were all paused and watching. Mei-Lynn finally turned the music off and there was silence. 'Give us some Bach, please,' Elizabeth said. '*Sonatas and Partitas.* Monica Huggett on violin.' The girl's organs moved with her breathing. Richard had his finger on the other cut. The music began, and they watched and then the blood in her rose again. She was still bleeding and it was then they saw the bright overflow pumping from nothing in the wide, strong ribbon of the psoas muscle.

'That's not the IVC, that's the lumbar artery bleeding.'

Elizabeth took up the needle and sutures and she held the muscle in one hand. She examined it. She leaned back and selected forceps from the tray and leaned in. She began to suture the lumbar vessel deep within the muscle by feel.

It was all very quiet as they watched her work. There was the gurgle and grind of suction, then quiet, and she spoke normally and taught them.

'This is a controlled emergency and not a chaotic emergency. The torrential bleeding from the vena cava is controlled with clamps and we can move in order of urgency. Richard has control of the posterior tear with his finger. The bleeding lumbar vessel is the most urgent due to the volume of bleeding and I am going to focus all my energy on that right now. Anaesthesia are you caught up?'

'I'm not sure.'

'We have a cut in the posterior abdominal wall from an uncontrolled trocar insertion that is controlled with digital pressure. We have a rent in the IVC which is clamped, and we have severe lumbar bleeding in the psoas that is posterior and deep I'm currently sewing with five-oh prolene,' she said.

'Thank you.'

As she sutured the others watched. Josie gathered the unused equipment. As she sutured Elizabeth whistled and hummed along with the Bach, little progressions that interested her, that moved her, and she murmured, *who*, quietly, now and again. As she pulled it off. As she nailed it, as she killed it.

'*Who*.'

When she finished sewing the lumbar bleed she sewed the

cut in the vena cava closed in seconds, and Robin unclamped it and as the blood flowed again the vessel swelled full and did not leak, and then she sewed the hole that Richard had been holding with his fingertip for 20 minutes. They hardly spoke during this part of the procedure apart from once, when Elizabeth said, 'How much blood,' and Robin checked the bottle on the suction machine and said, 'About 1400 mills' and held the big red bottle up. Vladimir said, 'A lot.' Elizabeth told Mei-Lynn to call and cancel the stump revision she had been scheduled to do and then she removed the IUCD and then she removed the girl's appendix for good measure. Then they went on with the original operation. They mopped out the pus and washed the girl's abdomen out with 5 litres of sterile saline. They closed up the wound with surgical staples and Elizabeth left Richard to sew up the port holes like a med student. They were finished at 5 p.m. with time for Elizabeth to have a cup of coffee and make her next operation at 6 and write up her notes afterwards. She visited the girl in ICU about 11 p.m. that night before she went home and the girl was awake and taking oxygen through a CPAP mask she didn't like and then she died at 4 a.m. the next morning.

The US Space Shuttle *Challenger*, like all the space shuttles of the late 1980s and early 90s, was comprised at launch of three main parts known in the business collectively as 'the stack'.

These three main parts are the shuttle itself, known as the orbiter, mounted at launch on top of a gigantic tank of fuel for the shuttle's engines, in turn flanked by two solid rocket boosters, or SRBs, to propel the stack into space.

Two minutes after launch those solid rocket boosters jettison, at 45 kilometres in the sky, and they descend by parachute to the ocean, where they are retrieved, refurbished and re-used, like sterilised surgical instruments.

The SRBs look like pencils and they are 45 metres long and weigh nearly 600 tonnes. Most of that weight is their fuel, a rubbery solid material made of ammonium perchlorate and atomised aluminium powder called APCP.

Because of the weight of the SRBs they are built off-site in four sections by a contractor named Morton Thiokol, huge drums moved by truck and rail to be assembled near the launch pad. Each section of rocket is joined to the other using a simple joint, known as a tang and clevis. A U-shaped joint, running around the perimeter of the rocket, which receives a tongue—the tang—from the section beneath. There are, necessarily, minute gaps between that U and that tongue.

APCP burning at over 3000 degrees Celsius finds that gap.

So at two points thin rubber O-rings circle the rocket. These two O-rings are just 6.4 millimetres thick and they sit inside a groove in the joint that is under 8 millimetres wide, greased and protected by flame-retardant putty. When the booster fires, the heat and pressure forces the O-rings into the gap between the tongue and the clevis. This is called pressure actuation. The rubber changes shape; it is forced to, and the forcing creates the seal necessary for the rocket to function properly. The launch thrust shoves the tongue up into the U and the O-rings into their grooves and the rocket seals up tight under pressure of a thousand pounds per square inch. It's all designed to move dynamically. To change as it plays. To adapt to the pressures it will face in a dynamic and predictable way. The stress is necessary for success.

When rubber is cold it is less flexible. Cold changes materials from a flexible, supple state to a hard and brittle state. The polymers are not moving. On the day of the launch of *Challenger*, January 28, 1986, it was 2 degrees Celsius. Part of the right-hand SRB faced away from the sun and there was a 6-degree Celsius difference between that side and the light. Each O-ring sits in a groove under 8 millimetres wide. They need to bounce back to seal that gap.

At just 0.678 seconds into the launch cycle there was already evidence of black smoke appearing above the O-ring joint on *Challenger*'s right solid rocket booster.

Meeting the parents

Elizabeth entered Wellington Hospital again at five the next morning through the great glass doors from the roar of windy darkness to lit calm.

The children of a young Māori family were climbing over the couches outside the elevators and the parents watched her as she came and when she grinned and said mōrena loudly the woman visibly frighted and Elizabeth punched the up button.

On the third floor she changed into scrubs and talked to Vladimir who had seen and consented the first patient already. In the wards it was very quiet with the ward lights still dimmed and the hospital still felt quite new, the wide surfaces and bare off-green walls. Here and there the orphaned posters telling everyone to observe the five moments of hand hygiene.

The glassed nurses' booth was half empty and uncluttered and Richard was waiting inside. He was smiling with the nurses and hunched over a clipboard. One of whom must have said his name or her name because his smile disappeared and he looked up sharply—his big new sideburns, his premature balding, his red and wide and vulnerable eyes. Richard was from Otago and his father was a senior surgeon at Dunedin and he used, she knew, carmellose sodium to hide the tiredness, his pockets full of the little plastic vials, leaving the bathrooms with tears in his eyes. Richard was 26 years old.

'Ready?' she said when he came out.

'Yes, of course.'

He held the notes to his chest and stared at the floor and she waited and she raised her eyebrows. 'Sorry,' he started. 'Sorry—13,' and he indicated the way like a maître d' and she said she knew where it was and he dropped his hand and followed her a step behind until she said, 'Walk beside me, Richard.'

'Yep.'

'How are you doing?'

'I'm all right.'

'You sure?'

'Yep, yep.'

'Good. How did you hear?'

'Hear what?'

She looked at him.

'Richard, we lost the sepsis this morning. I was texted on the way in.'

Richard went grey. She could see him thinking. See him ageing, see him recede and age. The pattern baldness would progress. The wrinkles that would deepen and dry. He wasn't cut out for this yet and needed to change.

'Oh,' he said. 'Oh. No, I didn't know.'

'It's very disappointing. It's a bad outcome,' she said.

He thought and she watched him muster his response.

'She . . . oh. That's . . . in ICU?'

'In ICU, yes. The sepsis was too advanced. She was likely never going to make it.' She watched his face. 'You okay?'

'Yep, of course. Yes.'

'What do you think?'

26

'The . . . trocar though—'

How much mercy do you need? She thought what to say. How to let him hang from the hook and still function. How to learn to love the hook.

'This was advanced sepsis, wasn't it,' she said. 'We can't know to what degree if any the extra time in surgery contributed.'

'But I suppose the complication—'

'—the complication contributed. We can't know how much. It certainly didn't help.'

He flinched then and she regretted it. She looked at him.

'We can't know, Richard,' she said, softer.

'No, I suppose we can't but—'

'We will learn from it. We will be better. Let's get on.'

'Yes. Okay.'

The morning's first patient was a double amputee, right and left legs, a white woman, 69, and she was sat up in bed with her prostheses off and her husband in the other chair under the window by her right side.

They were retirees from the South Island, following their grown children north. Living in an apartment on the flat in Petone. She had, at half past five in the morning before her procedure, done her hair. She was pale and a bit frightened and Elizabeth looked at them and chose a tone for their frankness, for their Southern hard.

'How are you this morning, Mrs McLean?' she said. 'Not too nervous?' She tilted her head like a caring and compassionate person would.

'Oh, no, no,' the woman said, and she smiled and pursed

her lips ironically at Richard. Involving the junior, bringing him in.

The husband was apart from them and he grinned and straightened his back for the doctor and already he looked disappointed. Elizabeth could see from his posture he was hearing impaired. He was eager to speak and control the conversation but he didn't.

'My name is Elizabeth Taylor, Mrs McLean,' she said louder, 'and I am the surgical consultant and this is my registrar Richard Whitehead. We'll be performing your operation today.'

'Hello.' The woman looked at the husband and feigned a look of fright. Then she smiled and the man grinned and grinned the pained grin of the deaf.

'How did you sleep?' Elizabeth said. 'Did you sleep well?'

'Oh, yes.'

'No, you didn't,' the husband said to her.

Elizabeth felt Richard look over at the man but she didn't look away from the woman.

'Well, you look very well this morning, Mrs McLean,' Elizabeth said. 'Did Eimear help you with your hair?'

It was unexpected and the room seemed to change. They stood apart and came into themselves. More than they had allowed themselves. And the husband looked at his wife and Richard came up into his skin again.

The woman smiled a bit, and touched her hair ironically, and she said, yes, she had, actually, and that it was a dry chemical shampoo in a cap, and wasn't it funny.

Elizabeth said, 'Eimear knows the tricks all right. Pay attention to what she says.'

As she said this she stepped around in front of the husband and extended her hand to take the woman's other hand, the

28

one that was not cannulated, to begin the examination.

The woman lifted her hand and it was offered and Elizabeth took it as if they were to be married.

Richard's face was still and calm and his body was at ease and still and she liked this. The patient will judge you, her consultant John Atelier told her in her FY2 year in London, not by the diplomas and certificates on your wall but by the manner and ease with which you perform the least manoeuvre. Elizabeth slid her left hand to the woman's inner wrist to take the pulse rate, rhythm and volume. A history of hypertension and aspirin to thin the blood that she'd not taken for 48 hours now pre-op. Elizabeth's hands were as dry as the woman's skin and they were the same warmth. She held the woman's fingers lightly in her palm. The pulse was light thunder, father in boots in the hall upstairs. The woman was to undergo a stump revision on both left above-knee and right below-knee amputations, performed seven years ago after a car accident. She had bony spurs rubbing through the repaired skin flaps, causing pain in her prostheses. They were going to cut the stumps open, file down the bone spurs and sew it all up again. The woman had requested pictures be taken. She was scared but knew what to expect. Elizabeth turned her hand over and drew her own wrist up alongside the woman's fingers as if to check her watch but it was to look for any signs of cyanosis along the flanks of her fingertips against the colour of her own skin. She turned the woman's hand again, looking for islands of redness on the pale palm: palmar erythema. An old working-class white woman with soft hands, elevated somehow. Too gentle for her world. Elizabeth rubbed her thumb under the knuckles and said, in a voice, 'What am I looking for?'

'Dupuytren's contracture,' Richard said hoarsely, and cleared his throat.

'Curse of the Vikings, they call it, Mrs McLean,' she said, 'who took it to Scotland where we find it among those poor bagpipers of the 15th century,' and laughed loudly looking the woman right in the eyes and the woman laughed back. 'Then it's very natural to extend the hand up to the epitrochlear node,' Elizabeth said, and she slid her hand along the woman's forearm to the elbow and though the woman was now quite calm the husband was looking increasingly alarmed.

Through the blue halls from patient to patient, on industrial lino in the blue dim before the lights came up, they continued their rounds. When they got back to the nurses' station the unit manager was waiting in his third-best suit.

'Morning, Liz,' he said. 'Good morning, Richard.'

'Morning, Alastair,' she said.

'Morning,' said Richard.

'Ha ha. What did you think of the new staff photo on the website?'

'Looks like a line-up from Nuremberg in their prison fatigues,' said Elizabeth. 'About to be taken out and shot.'

'Oh. Well, perhaps it was the black and white. We thought it might be nice to have everyone in a straight line. No hierarchies.'

'What can I do for you, Alastair?'

'Can we have a word, Liz?'

'What's this about?'

'Thanks Richard,' Alastair said.

'Thanks, Richard,' she said, and smiled at him.

'Sure,' he said, and he looked at Alastair before he left them.

'Can we go on in—' Alastair said, and he pointed away down the corridor.

The nurses watched them go from behind the glass.

'Are you headed to Queenstown for the conference, Liz?' he said in his office. 'Bit of a jaunt?'

'I'll go, Alastair. I'll take that one for the team.'

'Ha ha. I'd like for Richard to go along at least for the weekend and take someone from nursing.'

'Robin,' she said.

'Ah. Certainly.'

'Well.'

'Well it should be very interesting shouldn't it?'

'What should?' She grinned, just her mouth.

'The, uh, talk by the big Texan what's his name. In Queenstown. About publishing our results.'

'Publishing my results.'

'Well, absolutely. Yours. You're responsible, ultimately, under this proposition. The minister's mistake, they're calling it.'

There was a pause and they smiled at each other.

In three months the Minister of Health, a retired doctor himself, was to launch a system of open public reporting of the 'results' of New Zealand doctors and surgeons with a ceremony at Te Papa. These results were the fates of their patients, or 'outcomes'. This public reporting was to be of the outcomes of each surgeon alone, and the plan was to name those surgeons, like they'd done in the UK, in New York state. This year this surgeon killed seven patients. His name is John Smith. For

31

example. No one knew yet how it would look or where it would appear, despite the ceremony, the dinners—what paper, pdf, what url.

They all knew that in six months the minister would face re-election with the fallout from this scheme yet to settle upon the hospitals, but on campaign he'd have this claim to trot out, this claim that he had opened New Zealand healthcare to those who use it. That he had dragged New Zealand into 21st-century public service transparency. It was a bomb he'd dropped and a claim intended to win over patients and their votes, over the protests of their doctors—thin-skinned, he called them live on TV3—the thin-skinned versus those they had inadvertently skinned.

'It's the effects on training I think about, Alastair,' she said. 'For the young surgeons we're trying to teach.'

'The effects on training are potentially important.'

'What incentive is there for me to let my registrar try anything challenging if it turns to custard and goes on my stats?'

'Well, absolutely.'

'Absolutely meaning none at all.'

'Well, yes. Yep. You can certainly see it like that.'

They smiled and smiled at each other.

'Anyway, Alastair?'

'Well, look, Liz, the parents of the girl who died this morning have asked to see you. They're here now.'

'Oh?'

'Look I warn you they're very distraught.'

'I'm sure they are.'

'They were under the impression that when she was admitted yes it was an emergency but appendix or something like that. They've been caught very off-guard and they say they weren't satisfied with the explanation ICU gave them.'

'Who spoke to them from ICU?'

'Ben Matthews. Ben was her intensivist.'

'Well.'

'Well I hate to ask, but.'

'Why? She was my patient. I'm happy to talk to them, Alastair.'

'Your contribution to the running of this unit is invaluable, Liz. Your contribution to this hospital. What you bring to the table. You are integral,' he said.

'Oh shut up. I'm happy to talk to them.'

'Of course. Well.'

'Well?'

'So. Well—what are you going to tell them?'

'I'm going to tell them what happened in surgery. I wasn't there for anything important in ICU.'

'What really happened, Liz?'

'You've read the notes. You know what happened.'

'Uncontrolled insertion of a trocar leading to ... some internal damage.'

'Unrelated to the galloping infection that led to her fatal deterioration in ICU.'

'Unrelated,' Alastair said, and watched her.

'That's what I said.'

There was nothing else in the room but a desk and a PC beside a round table with two chairs, some tissues and a yellow sharps box. On the wall was a clock and a calendar showing the wrong month and a print of a painting of a boatshed.

The parents were sitting on the lip of a small sofa.

'Hello,' Elizabeth said. 'My name is Elizabeth Taylor. I was your daughter's surgeon yesterday afternoon.'

The woman's lips were heavily swollen and she was still crying and pale and not much older than Elizabeth herself. The man sat erect with his right arm around her. Her hand at her knee was shaking and her head wobbled and the man stared and moved his stare and stared.

'Owen Williams,' he said. 'This is my wife, Tessa.'

'May I sit down?' Elizabeth said and they didn't say anything and she pulled one of the vinyl chairs out from the table and turned it around and sat facing them. She was conscious she was higher than they were but there was nowhere else to sit.

'I am very sorry for your loss,' Elizabeth said.

They looked at her and waited. When she didn't say anything else they looked away. She could see the girl's blond hair in her mother. She remembered the father's wiriness in the girl's body under her hands.

'Thank you,' the father finally said, shaking his head slightly.

'Who has spoken to you?'

'Everyone but you,' the father said. 'The intensive care doctor, and a nurse and a counsellor who was bloody useless and that chappy I don't know who was from the DHB.'

'Here's what happened to Lisa,' Elizabeth said. They looked up at her. 'Lisa was very sick when she came to hospital. Some of her reproductive organs were infected and we think this was because of her IUCD. That stands for intrauterine contraceptive device. She had developed what we call sepsis, which is a very severe and life-threatening infection. We needed to do what is called a laparoscopy. That's a kind of keyhole surgery where we use a small camera to look inside Lisa and see what was wrong with her. During this operation we could see she was very sick. Many of her abdominal organs were infected—'

Their faces were changing as she spoke. She could feel her own face emptying as she confronted their destruction.

'—and during this laparoscopy it became clear that Lisa needed a proper operation to help her get better. I can tell you the details of that if you want.'

The man was clenching his teeth and blinking deliberately and controlling his face. The woman was building to something. Something mounting visibly in her that kept finding new levels and falling and rising again. They weren't saying anything and she had no idea if anything was being communicated.

'There was a complication in the surgery,' she said, 'and we needed to make a larger incision—'

She knew she had gone wrong then. The father sat taller and his eyes began to move quickly left and right, his blinking faster.

'—we were asked to sit outside the door,' the woman suddenly said.

'Okay,' said Elizabeth. 'I think that might have been in the intensive care unit. I've been talking about Lisa's surgery before her time in intensive care.'

The parents just stared at her.

'Let me try and explain. After I performed the operation to clean out the abscesses—'

'They said she had a heart attack,' the mother said. 'She's twenty-*four*.'

'Lisa had a very serious infection—'

'Why did it do that? Why did her ICD do that?' the man said.

She bore down.

'As I said, her IUCD had become infected. We don't know exactly why at this stage. There are many reasons this could have happened. Lisa was really sick. After her operation she was moved to the intensive care unit. I wasn't directly involved in her care there. Did the intensivist explain to you what happened there? Did Dr Matthews explain some of that?'

They were just looking at her in frank horror now.

'We thought oh her appendix must have burst for it to be that serious,' the mother said. 'They made us go sit outside. Jeany's driving down from Rotorua.'

'Is Jeany a member of the family?'

'Jeany is our other daughter,' the man said and his face was still with anger but there were tears and he was staring at her. 'She's got an I . . . U . . . CD too.'

Elizabeth said, slowly, 'I know this is really hard. Lisa had trouble breathing in intensive care. The infection was too much for her body. This led to her cardiac arrest.' She waited and she looked at them. 'Is Jeany going to come to the hospital?' she said more softly.

'Yes,' the father said, and shook his head.

'Do you all have somewhere to stay together?'

'We're in a motorhome,' the father said. 'At Kaitoke Park. She was camping beside us in the tent. With Stuart. We're just in a motorhome. We're not *from* here.'

'Do you want the staff to organise a motel for you closer by? We can find a motel nearby, or elsewhere?'

They stared and stared. The clock ticked. The woman's mouth hung open and she turned slightly to her husband. The man's eyes tracked back and forth across the carpet. Then they whispered together a moment, then they stopped.

He looked up.

'What's your name again?' he said.

'My name is Elizabeth Taylor,' she said, and smiled.

He reached into his pocket and took out his iPhone and touched the screen a few times.

Then he raised it and he took her picture.

She left the hospital at 10 p.m. into the surprise of windy misty night. The first rain in forever. The streets were empty and dark apart from the lights always on at Ronald McDonald House. Traffic lights all green through Newtown. She bought some half-price rotisserie chicken and mayonnaise and capers and a stale baguette at Countdown and she looked down Adelaide Road towards town and thought about renewing her CrossFit and knew it was pointless and she thought about the RACS conference in Queenstown in a few days, and then Vladimir's posture, suddenly, at the anaesthetic machine, and how she liked it, his straight shoulders and his slim hips and his patience.

She walked the other way up Adelaide Road towards the house and she was soon desperate for the toilet and it sullied her calm and she stepped and stepped at her doorway, feeling in the bottom of her handbag for her keys snarled in all the ribbons of her lanyards.

The house was a railway cottage, built in 1881 on the ridge above the flat stretch of Adelaide Road before the hill to MacAlister Park. Less than a kilometre to Wellington public, half that to Wakefield and the Southern Cross private hospitals. Perfect, easy for a surgeon, to do the public work in the morning, and pay off the mortgage in the afternoon. Pregnant, 19 years ago, she had torn up the carpet and ripped out the hardwood interior linings in the long narrow hallways by hand. Piled it all in the tiny front yard. There were layers of wallpaper underneath she'd stripped to get to the sarking but before that was a layer of newspaper from 1881 glued to the hessian scrim. Still readable. She'd ripped out a well-studded cupboard that hid a corner of pretty stained-glass windows, hearts and roses, that she could see in the exterior but were nowhere to be found inside. Nails so old the heads popped off in the claw hammer. She had to buy what her father called a jimmy bar to get under the timber. She hired a floor sander and sanded the kauri floors of all three bedrooms and the hallways herself. Mixed the sawdust and polyurethane into a glue she scraped into the gaps between the floorboards. She bought a haircap and kneepads and 3M goggles and used a surgical mask from work and went down under into the crawlspace through a small and crooked wooden door in the foundation. Alone down there, two days on her back on the dry sour dirt, she insulated under the tightly fitted kauri floorboards with bales of glasswool she stapled to the joists. Each staple sending clouds of borer dust from the tōtara uprights down upon her, where it congealed into a paste on her face in the sweat from the heat of the halogen lamp, $49.95 from Mitre 10.

As she peed and then as she sat and thought in the quiet of the house she resutured the cut in the artery in the girl's psoas muscle.

She was calm and very tired and she thought she might dream it again tonight. The girl's thin red muscle opening cleanly. The slack white skin around the incision brown with povidone-iodine. The sutures gathering the lips of the wound. Ordering the error, reshaping the artery, gathering its meaning. And the theft of that glory, that could not be enjoyed until later, now, here, on the toilet. The joy of work that could only be lost within, anticipated, and recalled. You want to live in that moment but you can't. Her face calm, a child on a lake somewhere, 15 days in the country. While a kilometre away in the morgue the wound did not heal and the body did not recognise itself, nor gather itself to itself, nor rise again. She sat on the toilet with her first finger and thumb gently clasped, dipping and dabbing and darning.

She went through her team and she felt good. Richard, Robin, Vladimir, Mei-Lynn. She liked it and they were strong and they had recovered and coped and even excelled. And as if her guarded comfort were a warning she thought past how she would feel if it were disturbed and the team disrupted or scattered, how she could use this lesson and this moment to salvage this dynamic and make it persist past the problem of people.

Outside the wind blew and the old house cracked. Robin had left her toothbrush in the jar. The streetlight through the trees and the stained glass of the bathroom window made a strange camouflage that flexed across the wall.

A sudden burn of peppermint in her mouth. She thought of the sutures dissolving in the dead wounds. In the morgue the cuts would drape open. The vessels sag and stiffen. All the work unwinding in the freezer. *Lisa Williams.* Her irises gone silver-blue and the eyeballs slack in the sockets. What a name. What was her middle name? She didn't know her middle name. She tried out some that might fit. *Jocelyn. Lisa Jo Williams. Sophia. Marie.* For the rhythm. *Lisa Marie Williams.* Her hair cold to the touch on the tray.

She thought of the Petone woman's pulse and of her father's good British boots, made by Tricker's. She'd bought this house with her inheritance as deposit. Her father had died thinking his daughter was a doctor and was going to have his grandchild. She thought of the heat of the cheap Mitre 10 halogen bulbs, and the costs for halogen throughout the DHB. She thought of the way you cut insulation—against the stud it would butt against. Hard against the thing that shapes it and holds it in place. She thought of other cases. She thought of Richard's sutures on the skin flaps of the Petone woman's stump. They'd filed down the spurs with the surgical rasp and before they closed she'd buried the nerve deep, deep with her forefingers back inside the muscle to dull the pain that would come. But suddenly she didn't like it—the old woman's skin was slack and thin and freckled lightly over fishbelly white—and she was suddenly sure the stump flap wound would infect and she was angry about it and she wiped herself and rose and put on her pyjamas and stood in the living room.

She had stripped the scrim and sarking and the cloth binding herself, and wired and insulated the walls and gibbed it herself, all but one wall, and she looked at the gib plasterboard as she ate her mean sandwich standing at the counter, searching out errors, unevenness, in the screwed and taped and stopped-up seams of the plasterboard, looking for the flaw.

What's not so well known about the fact of the cold O-rings on *Challenger* is other forces, other contingencies.

The launch had been delayed so many times. July 1985. November 1985. January 22, 1986. January 23, 1986. January 25, January 26. January 27 was postponed due to high winds. There was urgency to go. The shuttle was over time and over budget. They were carrying the Spartan satellite to observe Halley's Comet, which would not be seen from earth again until 2061. It was cold on January 28, 1986, and the wind shear at 45,000 feet was high; high, though within the limits measured and allowed.

The burning fuel escaping through the gap left by the cold O-ring in the right-hand rocket was quite visible on camera later. Black puffs of smoke that became a plume of fire as the O-rings vaporised, kilometres in the air.

But a by-product of the burning APCP was a crust of aluminium oxides that plugged the hole. It was sealed. The rocket burned on and the shuttle climbed, and climbed straight as it ought, with a good roll. Into the high winds aloft where, when *Challenger's* computers automatically adjusted to the lateral forces of those freezing winds, the scab cracked open.

If the winds had not been high the seal might have held through burnout, and the SRBs would have separated, fallen silent and descended through the atmosphere by parachute to be retrieved from the Atlantic and towed back to Canaveral by ship. It would have been found and shared and learned from, how close they had come to something utterly unknowable.

Jessica

That night Elizabeth dreamed of Jessica, tall in silhouette, turning and turning away from her in hallways where the boxes were stacked, because Elizabeth was moving house.

She woke early in the dark and lay and listened. Key in the front door. Grind of the latch. Steps in the hall, quick and light. The wind had stopped and the house cracked at the footfalls. The toilet flushed. The door opened and Robin came in naked and pale and carrying her clothes. She walked hunched to the closet. So-silent nurse. Elizabeth watched her body bend in the glow of the Adelaide Road streetlight, and the moles the size of wedding rings rough as cinnamon on her lower back.

'Hey,' Elizabeth said. 'Awake.'

'Sorry,' Robin whispered.

'Nah.'

Robin put on her pyjamas. Elizabeth pulled up a little spare duvet for her.

'Get a taxi?'

'No.'

'I said to this late,' Elizabeth said.

'It's a nice night.' Robin took a long breath and sighed. 'No words left,' she said. 'Up at six.'

'I'll speak to Alastair tomorrow.'

'No, my decision.' Robin rolled over. She lay there, then grunted gently, and shifted in the bed. 'You can't do stuff like that. It'd ruin things. They'd move me.'

'Ruin things.'

'It might.'

'He needs to be reminded.'

'It doesn't mean we go round holding hands. It's not him anyway it's nursing.'

Elizabeth sighed.

'We have to be careful,' Robin said. She shifted again, and then was still. After a while she said, '*So* not hungry.'

'Got some chicken,' Elizabeth said.

'Maybe for breakfast.'

'Might be a bit suss,' Elizabeth said. 'Dunno.'

'Dunno, dunno,' Robin said. She sighed again. 'Dunno.'

It was silent.

'Night, girl,' Elizabeth said.

She was already asleep.

The next morning, her first day off with no on-call in forever, Robin was already gone. Elizabeth got up and in her pyjamas sat at the kitchen table with a cup of coffee and wrote a thousand words for the peer reviewers for the *Royal London Journal* paper with Andrew McGrath.

She wrote for an hour and a half in the quiet house. She described her work like it was a procedure, an operation. She wrote that what ultimately happened for the patient, whether they lived or died, whether a prostate resection meant a man got his erectile function back or exactly how painful a hip replacement was six weeks or six months later—it was because of a team. Not just one person, one surgeon. But a team, even if the lead surgeon was in charge of that team. That the results of surgery depended on the patient's other conditions and the hospital in which the operating team worked. How they were cared for afterwards. She described the process of publicly reporting a surgeon's outcomes as ripping off a dressing again and again to check on the healing of a wound. She referenced it thoroughly. She used 'he' for her hypothetical surgeon throughout and quoted Onora O'Neill from memory: 'Plants don't flourish when we pull them up too often to check how their roots are growing.' She googled that line and she'd remembered it perfectly. She went on and on and it was unstructured and odd as a response to peer reviewers and she wrote it with no sense of whether it was something else or where to publish it, or to whom she might send it. Then she stopped writing and made tea and looked at the screen and frowned with a pained smile at what she'd done. She went through it all and changed he to she. She sat and looked at the screen and sipped from her cup. Then she googled Lisa Williams.

A self-proclaimed psychic, the first result said, a medium and healer who starred in two shows on Lifetime TV. Lisa Williams is a magical English woman living in Los Angeles. Lisa Williams is a Qantas Media Award-winning business journalist and marketer. Ten years' experience in planning and traffic engineering. Be the first to find out about Lisa Williams. Sent the card telling her children that she loved them before she was found badly burned at Newry Beach in Anglesey, Wales. Is a physical education professor. Is raising funds for Life with Lisa Williams on Kickstarter. Is an international heroine in her innovative efforts to counter child sex trafficking. Lisa Williams is a fraud.

She googled Lisa Marie Williams and Lisa Jo Williams. Lisa Marie Williams has an extensive career and Lisa Jo Williams is on Facebook and she searched Facebook for half an hour and then she googled 'Lisa Williams was' in quotes. Lisa Williams was born in 1973. Was live. Was described as 'beautiful' by her family. Was honoured as a 'Woman of Worth' by L'Oréal. Was still not convinced that she was really sorry or even had any remorse. Was found by a security guard. Was four years old.

She eventually stopped herself and cleared her browsing history and went out and stood in the garden.

When she came back in she started her reading and she wrote up some notes and then suddenly it was 3 p.m. and she hadn't even had her usual run and she had to think about going out. It was Saturday night. Ryan Adams was playing at the Opera House. It was hot and sunny and she was going out with Jessica.

Showered and changed, Elizabeth Taylor taxied to the biggest, whitest house on St Michaels Crescent in Kelburn and texted Jessica from the car as they had agreed. So she didn't have to talk to Jessica's husband Stephen, who was only 40 years old and had been made a district court judge two months ago. She didn't want to talk to him and she didn't want to have to deal with their kids either but Jessica wasn't outside when the taxi pulled up. She sat back and waited and stared at the house. Her heart beat lightly.

They'd had it professionally stripped and painted. Taken right back to the raw timber, she knew it cost them nearly $50,000 for the exterior painting alone. There were a few square metres of picket fences on weird angles at the street to cope with the slope outside. A crooked little garden of roses. But down the hill in the back of the house where you couldn't see it from the street was a kind of high-bourgeois paradise of terraces and bricked patios and concrete outdoor furniture and a pizza oven and play areas and even a flying fox. She could feel her face settling into a mask and her concentration narrowing to a still point—there were finials and chrysanthemums and a brass knocker on a great red door—and she paid and got out and went and took the brass knocker, let it fall.

She heard the scrabbling of claws and barking inside. Their dog was a black lab named Atticus who had a dicky hip and Jessica had two children, a boy and a girl, and Elizabeth could not remember their ages. Stephen opened the door. He was holding Atticus back by the collar and he was wearing a pink Lacoste polo shirt and icewashed blue jeans with bare feet. She smiled as he held the dog back and he didn't look up at her but down at the dog and he said to it—'No, Atticus, no—'

'Hello Stephen,' she said.

'Hello, Elizabeth,' he said and he grinned and grinned. He was very buff and tanned. He said sorry about Atticus, that he was going deaf now and he gets surprised by visitors as if Elizabeth knew all about him and shared their great affection. 'Oh,' she said, and Atticus reared awkwardly in Stephen's hand. 'You look well, Stephen,' she said, as if it were a question and she didn't know why, and he said, 'As do you, all flash for the girls' night out,' and he meant he knew he was handsome

47

but he was charming too. It was just a fact like others on his CV and that Elizabeth was Elizabeth, a clotted spiderweb of stuff like threat and ability and willpower, and she said, 'Shall I just wait outside,' and it was already fairly ruined.

'No no, come on in, can I pour you something as we're having some preliminary bubbles, preliminary to me babysitting but, ha ha ha.'

'Do you call it babysitting when it's your own children?' said Elizabeth and looked away around the room. Inside the house was all white walls and kauri floorboards and was filled with golden light from the sun wet over the Karori hills. There seemed an unlikely number of children roaming around. They ignored her like she was sending them a message to do so and she was.

'These aren't all mine, I don't think. *Otto*—' Stephen suddenly shouted at Elizabeth in exactly the same tone. 'Otto—take Atticus,' and a little boy came out of a cushion fort with his shoulders slumped and eyed her and sighed and took the dog by the collar. Stephen was grinning and he went into the kitchen looking away from Elizabeth and this was how you did courtesy, wasn't it, with people you don't like and who don't like you but are never going away, anywhere, ever.

'What did you paint the interiors in the end, Stephen,' she said to his back.

'Oh it's Resene Quarter Pearl Lusta,' he said.

He was waiting. He was waiting, she suddenly saw, as he poured her drink, for her to say something knowledgeable. Like oh for the warmth. Like oh it's actually whiter than the Spanish White isn't it, or oh it just glides on like maple syrup doesn't it, or something.

So instead she said, 'It looks great.'

He waited another moment and then he said, 'Well, I know

you would have done it all by yourself. I don't know how you find the time,' and she decided if she was going to do this she may as well do it properly.

'Congratulations on your appointment by the way,' she said, 'well deserved,' then here came Jessica down the stairs and she was resplendent, an insult in a black silk dress with a deeply carved décolletage and thin gold necklace at her heart and a spangled black clutch in one hand and she was tan and her hair was near black from the shower and tied back hard in a simple ponytail and she grinned at Elizabeth and Elizabeth smiled and Jessica was so obviously pleased to see her that Elizabeth had to look at other things. Stephen turned from Jessica to Elizabeth and then Jessica looked over the living room and shouted, 'Ruby, come on put the bloody train set away,' and then she turned back and her face was all dark and she said, '*Fuck*, Stephen.'

The sun was in the heights of the pōhutukawa over Aro Valley as they walked in and out of the shadows on the switchbacks of the dead stretch of Kelburn Parade. Elizabeth had worn flats because it was a concert, but Jessica was wearing silver heels and she'd taken them off and they were dangling from her fingertips and she was padding, tiptoeing down the rough paths. Elizabeth could smell the hot concrete and the dry macrocarpa and something small and dead and rotting in the bush and Jessica's perfume drying off in the last sun.

'My taxi driver's name was Lovedeep,' Elizabeth said.

'Pfft.'

'Lovedeep.'

'Why did he stop loving Eep,' Jessica said.

'I know. I know.'

'Because she sounds so nice. She sounds *so* lovely.'

The crickets buzzed and the streets were empty and they were both wearing big sunglasses.

Elizabeth, aware she was almost strutting, through empty Wellington suburbia, with Jessica. She could see Jessica's upper arm beside her and she was tan and the fine hairs were blond or transparent, and the muscle had softened with age but there was still that visible V in her triceps that she'd forgotten about but suddenly realised she'd known that V for more than 30 years and in a way that was a kind of ownership wasn't it, to have looked upon something age for 30 years. Who else could claim that. But you could choose to look at that or not to look at that and just not claim anything.

She looked away over the valleys and the gig was not till nine.

'It's been so fucking windy I've wanted to kill someone,' said Jessica. 'Would that help? Oh—' and she fumbled in her clutch for her iPhone and showed Elizabeth a picture of Atticus flat on his back with his legs spread, curled sideways in a quarter circle. 'The art of seduction, by a dog,' she said, and Elizabeth laughed with an exhalation through her nose and a hoiking sound in her throat, and they walked on.

After a while, Elizabeth turned to her in mock alarm and said, 'Oh, no—gin.'

Jessica stopped and turned to her and said, 'Fuck. *Fuck.*' Elizabeth could see herself in the big dark lenses and then they waited and waited, staring at each other, for the other to do something or laugh or come up with something and the cicadas howled and whined and then Jessica said who do you think you're dealing with and she opened the clutch and inside as well as the phone and some Party Feet and an eftpos card was her hipflask.

They sipped the warm gin walking down the hills into the shadows and by the crèche Jessica said cool it, that wouldn't be right, and they laughed. Forty-two years old, they were preloading on their way to Aro Valley for some ales before a concert, and it was sunny and warm and then Elizabeth did what she always did and she got too serious. She started talking about work and Andrew and Richard and her students and she talked about working on the editorial with Andrew and she said he's just such a walking pile of macho type-A privilege and Jessica said, '*You* are,' and Elizabeth laughed but then she didn't. She didn't say anything about Lisa and she never talked about cases. She talked about easy office stuff and Andrew and the Queenstown conference coming up and Jessica let her and Jessica listened and said, 'And you'd be almost literally like—' and she leaned her head back and shook it side to side, making a face, and went, 'Aaaaargh.' Elizabeth said, 'Oh God exactly' and then she explained the new legislation and public reporting of her outcomes and Andrew coming into the op and went on and on.

Jessica beside her tiptoed, nodding, her head inclined.

'What do you do in a situation like that,' she said.

On Devon Street there was the danger of people passing by who might overhear so she shut up and closed her face because everyone knows everyone and they walked on. Jessica took a huge swig of the gin and shuddered and said, 'Ay caramba, I need a friendly pint.'

The Taproom was full and before they went in Jessica tried to put her shoes back on. With a fingertip tugging on a heel strap, bent almost double with her tits all hanging out, on the footpath in front of Aro Café people were staring at her in her black dress and her wet hair tied back and her sunglasses and Elizabeth remembered she'd forgotten what it was always like, to be stabbed and sick and weak and bent and flabby, and she said, 'For God's sake woman, why are you wearing those.' Jessica said, 'I know, I *know*,' and she pulled them on awkwardly and tottered as she jammed the Party Feet into the heels. Then she stood up straight and she was 6 feet tall. She sighed at Elizabeth and made a face and Elizabeth smiled horribly back and Jessica just said, 'Oh shut the fuck up,' because she never got anything.

They sat on the stools by the mirrors opposite the bar and people pushed past them. A slim man with white hair in a denim jacket was leaning on the bar and he stared at Jessica until Elizabeth stared back at him and he laughed and turned away.

'Peter tells me these stories,' said Jessica. 'He tells me these stories about the minister. The minister, apparently, told him this thing about a certain issue I can't mention and then he explicitly says verbatim, oh but well, you know, that's just Māori boys being Māori boys. With a big laugh. In his position. He's not allowed to say or even think something like that. But "That's just Māori boys being Māori boys" he tells his staff. And Peter's like oh my God.'

'Back under Helen you couldn't fart without someone doing a pōwhiri,' Elizabeth said.

Jessica snorted. 'The hypocrisy is what gets him down apparently. Because behind closed doors that's just Māori boys being Māori boys.'

'Mmm.'

'It's outrageous.'

'Mmm.'

'Ban this sick filth.'

'Shut up. So who's Peter then?'

'Oh, we deal with him at ACC. Senior adviser in the minister's office. So bright.'

'Oh Jessica.'

'What.'

'Really?'

'What.'

'You know what it's called.'

'What what's called?'

'Pre-bounding.'

She'd already said it before she meant to because of the gin, and laughed to try and make it funny.

'No.'

'You have something of a record.'

'It's not even like that. I don't.'

Elizabeth snorted and looked away at the bar. Two boys, nearly 30, nearly 20, who knew anymore, had pints of chocolate stout and the barman was dipping what looked like a large soldering iron into their beer and it was hissing.

'It's none of my business.'

'No, it isn't, actually.'

They didn't say anything. After a while, into their silence, Elizabeth said, 'We should try one of those.'

Jessica looked. 'I haven't done anything yet,' she said to the bar. 'He's really understanding.'

'This is Wellington, Jess.'

'I'm being careful.'

'Oh well.' There was a long silence. 'I suppose you've got a plan for what to do about the kids.'

'Otto and Ruby will probably go with Stephen's parents until we've organised things. Peter's got a daughter and she's into ballet. Six.'

They were looking away from each other, at the soldering iron.

After a while Elizabeth said, 'Do you want one of those?'

Jessica reached over to the nearest boy and put her fingers on his wrist and said something to him and he offered her his pint to taste, almost giving it to her, giving it all away, grinning.

The other boy looked at Elizabeth blank as a cat. His right forearm had a new tattoo from elbow to knuckles and the hair on his arm hadn't grown back yet, or maybe the tattoo was old and he was still shaving it.

At the concert the Opera House was full and they were a little drunk and seated right at the back. Soon there were lesbians dancing in the aisles. A straight couple turned around and asked them to be quiet and got laughed at and Jessica called the man a cocksucker and Elizabeth stayed quiet because she thought she knew him from somewhere. Jessica and Elizabeth gasped and stared at each other when he sang the first lines of 'When the Stars Go Blue' and they gasped and stared at each other then when he covered 'Colorblind' by the Counting Crows. Then Ryan Adams played the first chords of 'Gimme Something Good' on his Flying V and it was so golden and right and their song and they stood on their seats and danced. When the drums came in Jessica slipped down between the cushion and the back of her seat and screamed and got her foot stuck and they laughed and laughed and she climbed back up again and they held each other and they sang *Gimme something good, gimme something good* into each other's faces and bobbed up and down and her back was so narrow and so hard it was sort of shocking and everything got luminous. But they were playing it too fast and then he played 'Do You Still Love Me?' and they climbed down and stood and listened and Elizabeth thought of Lisa and wondered if she was too young to even get this and if anyone young could ever like Ryan Adams and if it was just an accident of history that he became famous, and if Lisa was 24 she would like things so niche that Elizabeth couldn't even begin to understand the urge or attraction or accident of events that had led her to that artist. She found herself watching him and watching him as if she could squeeze him flat or tear him apart with his girlish thighs and his wealth and the way he flounced and was smiling. She remembered how he'd got Albert Hammond hooked on heroin and she remembered things she'd forgotten from high school and she started to remember she didn't believe he meant things and then everyone was standing up and she couldn't see him anymore, only his image on the pull-down screens at either side of the stage, and he was just the same there as he was on a screen on an iPad or something and he moved the same way and she couldn't feel anything. A man in the row in front of them was talking to Jessica now and afterwards Jessica told her that he knew where the band was going for drinks afterwards and did they want to go and Elizabeth was able to be amazed at her again, and she said no and in the taxi home all she could think about was the darkness behind the pulldown screen on which Ryan Adams was projected, the dark wings of the Opera House stage, and she hated him deeply, him with someone else's hair, him with someone else's voice, someone else's clothes, someone else's guitars, and she knew she would never go to another concert, for the boredom and the insult of the audience and performance and passivity and ease and that thin gap she could never fit through, into the wings where things were real.

Teaching

The most beautiful story of error I've ever read, Elizabeth liked to tell her students, is the timeline of the 86 *Challenger* space shuttle disaster.

I read it again and again. It's short and it's detailed and it doesn't patronise me. Some of the best writing of a complex physical phenomenon I've ever encountered.

It was assembled from shuttle telemetry, some internal shuttle and mission control comms, public NASA broadcasts and other stuff, and they edited it for shape. Two journalists. One they called a 'space correspondent' and a bureau chief permanently based at Cape Canaveral, which dates it nicely.

The cheering and the tower of light and smoke, the cold and the corkscrew of vapour collapsing in on itself and spreading like the skirts of a swooning actor in a period drama as she sinks to the sands.

Then the weird quiet and disappointment of the audience. Of all those who watch those who leave. The ambivalence seeping in. Odd moments of awe, staring up, but they're left behind, and then—

'That's not right. That's not right.'

'Get down.'

'Oh, my.'

Silence, and the roar of wind in the mic.

Then we pan up to the explosion.

The single trail swells and becomes two, curling wildly, becomes a pagoda of smoking streaked by debris like rain, and one long white streamer falling to the ocean. The smoke curling, reshaping, morphing. Then it all pauses, at an end, descending, compressing, and fading away.

Because there are simple problems, aren't there. There are simple problems, complicated problems, and complex problems. Simple problems are simple. Complicated problems are harder but they have solutions that are iterable. A solution works each time we encounter this problem. But a complex problem is different. A complex problem is a problem that changes as you play.

Is it a frog or is it a bicycle? she asked her students. Are you astronauts or engineers? Are you both? Are you managers too?

If you want to understand the implications of massive systems failure determined months in advance but happening in microseconds in front of you as you try to cope in real time the *Challenger* timeline is the first thing you might read.

There wasn't data to back up the case from the manufacturer that the cold temperatures on the day of the launch would inhibit the O-ring from moving to seal the gap as it was designed to do. I couldn't quantify it, said Roger Boisjoly, the engineer at the company that made the rings. I had not the data to quantify it, but I did say I knew that it was away from goodness in the current database.

The last reported communication from Michael Smith at 73 seconds is, 'Uh oh.'

Then: '*My God*,' says Kent Shocknek live on KNBC.

The Mission Control spokesman carries on reporting the trajectory of the debris as if it's still the shuttle flying, not the pieces. The band plays briefly on because they're not yet aware that it is already over; that it was already over when the Morton Thiokol engineers did not have the data to make the case to NASA management that at 30 degrees Fahrenheit the O-rings might not seal.

So, she said. There are simple problems, complicated problems, and complex problems.

And then there's just chaos.

Conference, Queenstown

When the keynote speaker rose to the podium and began to shuffle his papers Elizabeth was seated alone at her table, though every other table in the conference hall was full.

The anaesthetists and the surgeons were the men in suits with no ties. The nurses and anaesthetic techs were the women, and the women who were more senior wore pantsuits and the less senior wore T-shirts and smocks and even trackpants. Teams and hospital units sat together. Pink and hospital blue. The room was an abstract atlas of New Zealand healthcare: medical and surgical, upper GI, orthopaedic, vascular, neuro, cardiac, general; Northland, Southern, Capital and Coast. The teams and the units sat together and the surgeons and anaesthetists roamed the room, table to table, keeping up the chatter, showing their leadership, staying off their phones.

The nine other places at her table were empty. The debris of the long day strewn about. Conference programmes, Royal Australasian College of Surgeons goodie bags, pens with logos and abandoned mints in cellophane envelopes no one could open. Elizabeth leaned back and she looked up from her phone and raised her eyebrows as the Texan began to speak.

'I'd like to thank Andrew for his very flattering introduction and before I get on to figures and graphs and whatnot there's a quote I like a lot and it's been pointed out I seem to like to say it a lot.'

They tittered for him with good-natured New Zealand willing. The first PowerPoint slide flicked up. Elizabeth eyed it over her glasses.

Epidemiology is just people with the tears wiped away.

She looked down to catch Robin's eye at the Cap Coast nurses' table. They smiled fixedly at each other, without teeth.

Doctors spend an awful amount of time in lectures. They spend an awful amount of time with PowerPoint. Certain platitudes in medicine get a lot of PowerPoint use. The strategy of reminding everybody what they were all really here for had become its own cliché and it could work. It could be right. If you were old enough, if you'd seen enough. Almost the entire group gathered in the pearly, golden hotel for the RACS Queenstown surgical safety and measurement conference 2017—'Measuring What Matters' it read on a billboard on an easel—maybe 160 healthcare professionals, a good deal of the country's surgical community—would be gathered again at the perioperative mortality conference in April. Teams would be operating with each other again inside 36 hours. Applying for jobs. For RACS fellowships. CME points. Passing each other instruments and requesting letters of reference, letters of recommendation. You didn't roll your eyes in this company.

Elizabeth looked at Robin and rolled her eyes.

'Now what you all have decided to do, or what's been decided for you by your health minister and put upon you and hung over your heads, is a huge thing. A *huge* thing. A bitterly contentious thing let me tell you. You're going to start measuring and putting your surgical outcomes out there into the public sphere and you cannot expect it not to be. It's gonna be a shitstorm.'

The crowd laughed.

'But let me tell you this—it gets better.'

And then they really laughed.

'Ha ha, now look you've up till now—and you might find this hard to believe or imagine—you've been invisible to your patients. You *are* invisible to your patients. You come in there the day before or a few hours before they go under and they remember you but they are not going to remember what you say. And now you're gonna start telling Joe and Jill Public a couple of things they've hitherto been unapprised of.'

The down-home thing was an angle. He was a Texan but Director of the Division of Research and Optimal Patient Care at the American College of Surgeons and he spoke all over the world for huge sums and he was near-royalty in the profession and the media's sense of the profession. Flown out from Johns Hopkins on College coin and paid per diem. Demanded first class for himself, his wife and son, the rumour went, and the flights alone came to more than NZ$30,000. Wearing man make-up because this thing was being filmed. A star.

Elizabeth watched him, his quick clean hands, smooth and white from the scrubbing. His wattled chin and cowboy lean.

'Now all of a sudden under this new disposition you surgeons and your teams are going to tell them some very dangerous and risky material for their sense of what you are and what you are going to do to them when they go under your knife. First that this is not magic and this is not religion. They're gonna find that out when you publish these results. They're gonna find out that within 30 days of this impending operation of theirs they're already het up about that they have a 2 percent—or 12 percent, or 20 percent—chance of dying, and an X percent chance of getting some serious complication. That's okay. Your patient is not gonna have little or any sense of what that means. And it's not that relevant to them. There's a risk and they're already at risk. Please just be compassionate with me Doctor. Please just be a little bit kind and understanding. Take me by the hand and look me in the eye. Speak to me simply and clearly.'

'Why don't you speak to *us* simply and clearly?' Elizabeth said loudly.

Some in the crowd laughed. Robin looked down at the table.

The Texan laughed, and continued.

'But what they're also all of a sudden going to find out—whether they look it up or see it on a blog or in the paper or their kid who's up on big data tells them—is that this figure is not a blanket figure. Up the road is another man who can give them better odds: a 1 percent, or 10 percent, or 15 percent chance of dying.

'And that they cannot go to that surgeon. They *cannot.* That less risky bet is off limits because your system ain't built that way. You're not choosing a mechanic. Sorry about that.'

He was very confident and the folksiness had all but ebbed. They weren't laughing as he was speaking to the surgeons directly now, and their staff knew it.

'And you can sit there all serious and explain to your patient that the surgeon up the road the data say is hot shit is a young buck qualified for six whole months who's operated on a grand total of seven young white patients handsome and strong who never smoked a day in their life while you've been down in the trenches mopping up frequent fliers and the morbidly obese and the diabetic elderly brown folk with the

DVT risks and the histories of gout and falls and respiratory disease. You can tell them that till you are blue in the face. It won't fly. They are not going to be interested in the intricacies of risk adjustment. They are just not.'

The Queenstown sun was a pale gold thing, almost solid, an oblong hanging in the hotel air from the concourse windows through the double doors of the conference hall open against the heat. Elizabeth watched herself feeling that familiar uptick of fear. She called it watchfulness but she knew it for herself to be fear. Empty stomach, tick of her heart, chemical stench of peppermint, a huge calm. She tapped her pen tip against the table.

'So what can you do? The genie's out of the bottle. There's no going back. You're going to be ranked and you're going to be compared and it's going to happen publicly and in print and all your dirty laundry is going to be out there for the public display. Everyone who's died under your scalpel. Every surgical site infection. Every nicked aorta. Every dead dad.'

It was quiet.

'Some of you may be forced to leave practice or will leave of your own accord. This is not a bad thing.'

A dead silence.

'So I say what 2014 Democratic primary candidate for governor of Massachusetts, Don—21 percent of the vote, go Don!—Dr Don Berwick said after the big old Mid-Staffs scandal in the UK.'

Half the reference was lost on the room and there was no laughter apart from one horsey, inappropriate splutter at the vote.

'He said don't be afraid of being measured. He said don't be afraid of the light. He said get over the hump. He said all teach. All learn.'

Silence. Elizabeth was staring at the Texan as if she could see inside him.

'It's gonna get better cos *you're* gonna get better. You're gonna *want* to.'

He looked about and smiled.

'You're gonna *have* to.'

A blowfly wandered buzzing into the room.

'Hello?' Elizabeth said loudly.

Several in the audience turned her way.

'Excuse me?' the Texan said, and he shaded his eyes.

'Hello?'

'Yes?'

'Yes, hello,' she said. 'Liz Taylor.'

'Ah. Yes?'

'Yes, ha ha.' She made her face of My Name is Funny. He smiled down at her.

'What can I do for you Ms Taylor.'

'Mrs Taylor.'

He caught that she was a surgeon. '*Mrs* Taylor, I'm sorry.'

'Well I gather you're pro all this?'

'Well'—he laughed and looked around the room—'I'm pro-future because it seems to happen whether I like it or not.'

The room laughed. The New Zealanders looked this way and that as if they could fidget out of their embarrassment.

'Well, that's what I call resignation,' she said brightly. 'I'm just a bit meh on this to be honest. You've read the *Lancet* paper?'

'The *Lancet* paper?'

'Yes, the *Lancet* paper.'

'I read a lot of papers—'

'The *Lancet* paper puts it very clearly, Doctor. Walker and colleagues 2015. Look it up. We don't do enough.'

'I'm sorry, we don't do enough to prevent harm or—'

'We don't do enough *procedures*. There's not enough hours in the day. According to Walker et al. in the *Lancet* there aren't enough people in the UK for this, and look around— there certainly aren't enough people *here*.'

The group was now evenly divided between those who were staring at him and those who were staring at their tables.

'What we're talking about here is, I guess—'

'Look, sorry, I just want to continue a bit here without you thinking me tendentious or a bitch or anything because this is important to us.'

Andrew's head snapped up at the adjoining table and a senior anaesthetist at Middlemore beside him was now openly staring at her, shaking his head.

Elizabeth said, 'Look, there are plenty of reasons why we shouldn't be doing this and I'm not going to go through them all.'

Richard was smiling palely at her, his eyes wide.

'But what I hope we're all aware of are the effects this is going to have. Whether we wish it or not we will avoid sicker patients. You've seen this in the States. Why add this patient circling the drain to my numbers? Why take the risk? It's called risk aversion and you've seen it in the US and you'll see it here too. It will affect everything. It will affect training. Who wants to give their registrar a go in case everything turns to shambles and it goes on your numbers?'

The table around Richard froze a small second and didn't look at him.

'—Liz,' said Andrew, 'you make a good point, or points, but at Auckland they've been doing work with simulation and training—'

She leaned sideways to look directly at him.

'Exactly. At *Auckland*.'

Robin was sitting straight up at this, as publicly outraged as she ever got.

'If you mean resourcing—' said Andrew, blinking rapidly.

'Oh look,' she said. 'I mean numbers. We're talking about numbers, aren't we? So let's talk about numbers. The *Lancet* paper—'

'The *Lancet* paper—' Andrew said.

'Neoliberal data-diving is fine and dandy but we're talking about ranking people in public and driving them out of practice with insufficient data on how good they really are.'

She was losing the room. The fear and suspense was one thing. But it was the end of a long talky session and the novelty of the famous Texan speaker helicptered in to save the day had worn off. She had saved her speech for last and it was too late.

'We are scientists aren't we? Or technicians? Or are we just chancers? What scientist agrees to make a judgement and publish that judgement when he knows he only has an even chance he's right? Do you know what UK surgeons are asking themselves? When that sick patient comes in at the end of the month and they have to choose whether to operate or not, they ask themselves, *do I feel lucky*. They're doing about 130 cardiac bypasses a year each and that's a lot and it has relatively high mortality of about 1 percent. At 130 operations a year you have about an 80 percent chance of being right when you say someone has a normal number of deaths. Two times out of ten someone's killing people and you won't know it. This is called false complacency. Do I feel *lucky*.'

The Texan had been leaning on the lectern with weary determination. Andrew was signalling him somehow, because he straightened and said, 'Well, we appear to have moved into the Q and A slightly ahead of time—' and the room laughed, relieved.

Elizabeth breathed through her nose, and smiled horribly.

'We can't afford to be idiots about this and blindly follow the world. How many cardiac surgeons can we afford to lose? Do you know how many we've got?'

'Liz—'

'Twenty-nine.'

'Okay.'

'Not enough.'

'Okay, Liz, thank you.'

'Twenty-nine,' she said, and put down her pen.

'Okay.'

Now she was surrounded by an abundance of smiling women. They were gathered in the centre of the hotel concourse. They were perioperative nurses, infection control nurses, anaesthetic techs. They were charge nurses and ward managers, and these were the older, bigger women, dense and sizeable with responsibility and the things they'd seen.

'I was interviewed by a journalist from the *Sydney Morning Herald* back in the day,' Elizabeth was saying, 'and I told him, I tell all my female students that if you're approached for sex by a male colleague or a male superior you're better off just saying yes.'

There was a little quiet and the younger nurses laughed uncertainly. They checked each other, and they watched her. They had hors d'oeuvres plates with half-circle holes moulded in the rim from which to hang a wine glass by the stem to free up their other hand, but none of them knew or thought to hang their glasses there.

'True. You're better off just saying yes and getting it over with.'

Robin, standing beside her with a tall glass of iced water, looked pained.

'If you're approached in your off-hours or in the hospital or even at a conference like this you're better off in the long run just saying okay fine then and getting it over with.' Elizabeth stared at them until they began to stare back. 'Well? What do you think?'

They were quiet. The smiles were slipping, uneasy. She was matter-of-fact, maternal even. This group was dense with connection. Memories and hierarchies. Even checking someone's face was dangerous. There was so much history they could barely move.

'Just get it over with,' she said. 'In a closet. In a car. In the toilets of whatever bar or restaurant you happen to accidentally run into him. Quick as you can and none the wiser and move on, because otherwise, I'm not joking, it will follow you round the rest of your career. He will follow you round the rest of your career. This is an island. He will always be there and you will always be there and he will rise and you won't and you won't know why. So I'm telling you why. His power extends even to shame and his shame at being told no is worth more than yours saying yes.'

The sun poured over Ben Lomond through the concourse windows, glowing in the wine, setting the glasses to dazzle. They weren't smiling at all anymore. Their faces had changed but Robin's expression had not changed. Still patient, still pained.

Elizabeth said to the women, 'So I said to him, that's what

I tell them, and I stand by it. Of course everyone took it a bit literally.'

She burst into loud laughter and laughed even louder watching them and only some of the hard charge nurses who had seen everything laughed with her.

'Hello Liz,' said Andrew laughingly, beside her. 'How's our *Royal London* paper coming?'

'Oh, hello Andrew,' she said. 'Not bad. Peer review's a bit good cop bad cop.' The nurses stood by, suddenly shy. 'You all know Andrew. Head of surgery, dean of the med school now and still in clinic a day a week. I was just talking about teamwork, Andrew.'

'Ah, well. What did you make of the talk?'

'I don't know if it's enough, is it, Andrew?' she said. '"All teach, all learn." Easy to say.'

'No, I suppose it's not enough at present, is it.'

'People will be crucified.'

'Yes, they might be.'

'Seems like he's pro all this.'

'Well, as he says.'

'And here you're shepherding him amongst us.'

There was a silence. She liked that he came to her after the confrontation. She liked that he persisted. Andrew looked about the crowd and she saw him change his face.

'You're not worried about your own data?' he said. He grinned and laughed mincingly, leaning towards her then back again.

She smiled and breathed and looked around her. *Be careful.* The women had merged with the crowd. Andrew. Robin. Richard over there, heading for the exit. *Drifting away from land.* Jocelyn Chambers, the NHS change specialist there for the conference, was talking to a young, good-looking male periop nurse, touching her hair. Flirts and sharks. *They want to get inside you, transcend you. Rise above you. Burst you and be lifted. It is the real hidden curriculum.*

He offered another laugh at his own comment. He pronounced it, ha ha ha.

She didn't reply and turned away to her women. They were pairing off and receding, sharing war stories, horror stories. Eyeing the exits for a fag. She wanted to get back to the hotel, answer some emails, drink some more wine watching the mountains in the last light across the lake. Then a bath, and sleep in a big white bed.

'Well—no, I'm not,' she said.

'The cardiac surgeons have seen this coming for a long time,' he said.

And then she couldn't control herself.

'They've got a registry, Andrew,' she said. 'They've got ministry money. They're organised. They've got examples and models from all over the world. They've got pre-defined data dictionaries and clinical buy-in and dozens of data points being collected,' she said. 'They've sat on it for years. They haven't published anything. *Knowing*—'

But he had grown calmer, less solicitous in his manner. His face—blurring, pleased.

The closer to Caesar, the greater the fear. Drenched in the hatred. Don't be passionate. Don't be emphatic in these conversations and do not anger. Just be right.

'The other specialties are nervous, Andrew,' she said, calmly, as if it were something he'd overlooked. 'If they're collecting their data at all, they're sitting up at night filling in Excel spreadsheets in their singlets in front of *MasterChef*. Politely emailing graphs to each other. We're years behind the world on this. We're all recording different things.' He looked

71

at her. 'The generalists are nervous,' she said.

'Yes and to some extent rightly so. The *Lancet* paper—'

'Yes, the *Lancet* paper puts it very plainly.'

The shortening replies were attracting attention. They were in the centre of the room and the nurses had turned and were watching them, listening.

At sunset she raised her eyes to Robin and left the conference and walked down Adelaide Street to the lakefront and there was a park bench and she stood alongside it and watched the last sun ascend The Remarkables.

Walking home to a plush hotel in warm winds in twilight after three glasses of wine and a too-public event. To be alone.

The lake had gone silver-black and the pines above were dark and above them, as the sun behind her moved between a bank of cloud and the mountain ridge, the foothills bloomed like stage lights coming up and the pines darkened further. The great wreckage of the mountains was all impromptu lit a dirty glowing terracotta. The reflection filled the lake's still mirror and goldened and tarnished the entire valley of the lake. Then the ridgeline's shadow rose from the water and flowed up the gravel and the rock, a dark sarcoma blooming from the seam of lake and blackened pine, and it raced up the mountain and across the water towards her until the last light on the peaks was the only trace of colour left in a wash of white-blue suffusing everywhere as the day died.

She stood there, all stupid and overwhelmed. Weary of talk. Shear gradients, restenosis, percutaneous coronary intervention. Fuck landscape. She felt it: the hunger, the confidence of holiday: ready to get back to work. A tingling in her fingers, a pricking in her thumbs.

That night she dreamed of the operation again and woke in the big white bed in a copper stink with Lisa dead in the bed beside her bleeding from the eyes.

The astronauts and the ground crew talk on. Shuttle pilot Michael Smith shouts over the intercom, *'Feel that mother go.'* Someone unidentified shouts *Woo-hoo*, someone they'll never know. Plumes bursting from the rupturing O-ring become continuous now and internal pressure in the right solid rocket booster plummets. Flame from the fissure burns through the strut holding the rocket to the huge external fuel tank containing 550,000 litres of liquid oxygen and a million litres of liquid hydrogen as they hit Mach 1.9.

The strut burned through, the 600-tonne solid rocket booster swings wildly, attached only at the nose. The bottom of the hydrogen tank fails. The swinging rocket hits the external tank between the hydrogen and oxygen and it ruptures and the fuels mix and vaporise. This all happens in under a second. There is no shockwave. What we see in the sky isn't a true explosion but a cloud of smoke and fire and gases and the exhaust from the SRBs, engulfing *Challenger* as it moves at nearly twice the speed of sound.

Smoke, fire, gases, exhaust, and reflected sunlight.

The M&M

The monthly Morbidity and Mortality meeting was held on a Monday after hours as it always was, in the fifth-floor conference room they called Siberia—the last room on the end of the long, long corridor. The view was over the skyline of eastern Newtown to the villas, the old fever hospital up in the trees, and the mental health unit below. Closer by were the nine steel chimneys of the hospital waste disposal plant.

Siberia had a whiteboard wall but the whiteboard paint didn't work very well and the notes from five years of deaths and accidents remained pale and some of the words and numbers were still quite clear when they wrote up the notes of the new deaths and the new complications over the top. The room was full of men of all ages in suits, who were comfortable in their bodies, men used to their bodies, used to standing still in one place for eight hours at a time.

The piecemeal conference table they stood around was crooked and they stood among articulated boardroom chairs. Everything was adjustable so no single chair looked the same or sat at the same height or on the same recline. There was a sad twilight light out there and the far-off sound of traffic and Elizabeth came in hard and fast as she always did.

She used her folder of notes to push the door open and left it open and then she dumped the notes on the table, said loudly, 'Hello,' and stood behind her chair examining her phone. Women surgeons usually found two ways to be: they became men or they became something else entirely.

'Hello, Liz,' said Andrew from the far end of the room. 'Welcome.' The other men stopped and turned and smiled. 'How's that *London Journal* response coming,' he said and smirked. She looked up from her phone and she said, 'This one's personal.' They liked that and the men laughed. Robin and Vladimir came in behind her. Vladimir sat down precisely between her and the gathered surgeons and Robin sat on the other side of Vladimir.

One by one, in their own time, the surgeons went to their seats.

Nathan was first. He was a 30-year-old bariatric and general surgeon and social media zealot who had recorded a version of his registrar years on Twitter where everyone was inspiring and no one swore or was disgusting or cruel. He had a Hitler Youth short back and sides, a bow tie, beard, and a moustache with twisted tips. Elizabeth stared at him for an appalled second and the whole room paused and held. Risen on the balls of their feet when the light has changed, about to cross a road.

'Right, well, hello, a good meeting is a short meeting and I don't think there's a lot to get through here today,' said Andrew. 'I'd like to welcome everybody and thank you all for coming. I hope to have us out of here by half seven.' He smiled the smile of someone who decides: now smile at them. 'We've got nursing and anaesthetics here today as well as surgery and that's great to see.'

'I'd like to leave a little early m'fraid, Andrew,' murmured

Simon Martin.

'Likewise,' said Jason Latham, and laughed. The others made sour, smiling faces in their suits.

Elizabeth leaned forward and looked around the table exaggeratedly.

'Hold on,' she said. 'Where is Dr Matthews?'

Andrew looked at his notes. 'Uh, as some of you may or may not know, Dr Matthews was the intensivist on today's main case. Uh, a Lisa Williams.'

The surgeons reclined in the articulated chairs. Some of them swung back and forth. Nathan sat very upright. He was smiling and he sipped his Wishbone coffee from the vintage orange china cup and saucer he always brings from home and carries down to Wishbone to get his coffee. He always holds the cup in two hands when he drinks.

'Uh, Dr Matthews is an apology,' Andrew said.

There are things she hates she can't say and can't share. Men prepared to tell people they prefer to drink their coffee from china. Who act decisively on that preference. Elaborate male facial hair. New Zealand. An anonymous man she once overheard at a fertility clinic saying, I don't need to see that. He'd been asked to accompany his wife during the procedure to have her egg inseminated with his sperm returned to her uterus. All the female nurses and the wife herself laughing sympathetically for him. Lazy masking with two-dollar-shop masking tape. It leaves fillets of paint-soaked tape glued to the skirting boards. Two generations of New Zealand men now who think that opshop suits with flares and big lapels, fake moustaches and Elvis sunglasses, are funny, are fancy dress. How they hide to act strong and sure of themselves. The implications of that, evolutionarily speaking. Certain phrases. 'Kids love mince.' 'Cultural competency.' Baby boomer public

77

healthers who fell into professorships in the 1980s after decades of tagging themselves on to futile, well-meant public health promotion programmes, wasting their lectures and their students' time and money with anecdotes of boring long-past alcohol and tobacco campaigns, and adding their names to the publications of 25-year-old PhD candidates adjuncting themselves to death on a pittance with no benefits and doing all the work. Get made associate professor and make real money. Reunion concerts. Wasted time. Het men who make an elaborated point of the fact they don't care about fashion. Het men who make an elaborated point that they do.

'I'd like to call for this meeting to be adjourned,' Elizabeth said.

She pushed back her chair and stood, gathered her notes, looking down at her phone.

They swivelled in their seats to look at her.

'Uh, now, Liz,' said Andrew.

'Yes?'

'What's the story?'

'If Dr Matthews isn't here what's the point?'

'Well the point, Liz, is surgery and mortality,' Andrew said and laughed, but no one else did.

Jason Latham was staring at her.

'The *mortality* here,' Elizabeth said, 'is not *related* to the surgery. The *mortality* is related to the girl's advanced sepsis and the nearly 12 hours of intensive care that failed to save her afterwards. Without an ICU representative we are pissing about in the dark and we are going to get piss all over ourselves.'

Nathan audibly laughed with a half-contained spit through his lips and Jason turned away from her, smiling down at the table.

'Well, let's not get excited,' said Andrew.

'I'm leaving unless and until ICU get their A into G and turn up.'

'Liz.'

'Sort it out, Andrew.'

The surgeons were all looking in different directions and were, largely, smiling. Vladimir was expressionless and Robin was staring at the table.

'Liz, we need to address this. Look, we're not here to apportion blame.'

'*Blame*?'

'Look, Liz,' said Jason. 'You've got a point but where's Richard Whitehead? Why is your registrar not here?'

'He's caring for patients, Jason. Where's yours?'

'Mine's not one of the named subjects of a complaint to the DHB, that's where mine is,' he said and he smiled and leaned back staring at her.

There was a silence.

Elizabeth turned to Andrew.

'A complaint?'

'A complaint.'

'Is that a fact?'

'That's a fact.'

'The parents.'

'The parents and the uh, boyfriend have written to the DHB,' Andrew said. 'There is now an official complaint, yes.'

'When were you going to tell me about this complaint?'

'I'm telling you about it now.'

There was another silence.

'Then all the more reason this should be taken offline and ICU should be involved,' she finally said. 'That girl was delivered to them with a ribbon on top.'

Andrew looked away and his voice was soft.

'Liz, all the more reason for us to sit down and go through everything we can know about what went on that day and that night in a collegial fashion sooner rather than later.'

'Oh, don't be stupid,' she said.

Nathan picked up his cup and took a sip of his coffee and put his cup back down.

Jason was not smiling anymore. He was staring at her. 'Why do you call people stupid?' he said.

'Question sort of answers itself doesn't it?' Elizabeth said. She looked at him. 'Why aren't you laughing?'

'Now why would that be stupid, Liz,' Andrew said evenly.

'It would be stupid because we can sit here and go through my notes and talk to my team until you're blue in the face but you can't possibly know what went on with that girl unless you have ICU and their nurses here. From both shifts after my handover at 7 p.m. and before her death at 4 a.m. Because they took over her care and she died on their watch.'

Robin's mouth was closed and her eyes were moving from the tabletop to the middle distance above it and back. Vladimir had not moved.

'The complaint,' Andrew said softly, 'addresses the surgery. The complaint addresses the complications that occurred during that surgery. The complaint alleges certain errors by staff here, irregardless of the care she received in ICU and the contribution of that to Liz's death.'

He laughed.

'I mean, Lisa's death.'

Elizabeth laughed, and some of the older surgeons laughed too.

'*Irregardless*,' Elizabeth said.

'Regardless, rather,' Andrew said, and he laughed again,

differently.

Other things she hates.

Men from the past in Facebook photos. Standing around their barbecues in their straw hats, their Panhead IPA T-shirts, cargo shorts and black wrap-arounds. She can't remember who they are or distinguish between them. The women in chiffon and chambray sacks and big hats and sunglasses so huge she can't tell who they are either. The $7 folding camping chairs on the rude ragged lawns down south.

The two pictures of Kirsten Light. The only ones on her feed she has ever posted of herself without her children. All 6-foot-blonde of her. The first posted March 17, leaned back, awkward, with one arm up on a fence of concrete block. The second posted March 18, an exact copy cropped to cut off the small bulge of her belly. Half an hour fumbling with Photoshop but she'd left the original up. Her little southern vanity. She had gentle eyes and big front teeth and Elizabeth remembers buzzing around her like a fly for two years in high school. Wanting to hold her down and spread her legs and lick her from her ass to her cunt for hours. Until she emerged. Until she came out where Elizabeth was. When Kirsten Light realised what the little friendship meant she turned stone and ash and had a horsey sneer for her forever after. Went into nursing and never posts photos of her husband. Just those southern daughters with names like Neisha, Chanelle, Bianca. *That thing in my face that makes your smiles go away. That thing in my face.* Butter on buttered toast that melts too soon and completely. She likes those little lingering lumps of butter.

Elizabeth sat down.

'Okay,' said Andrew. 'Let's have eyes down looking.'

Elizabeth sat and looked down at the cover page of the

notes and didn't blink for a long time. On either side of her Vladimir and Robin didn't move. The surgeons flicked through the pages. The air conditioning hummed. Outside the day died and it grew dark and the furnace dissolved in the darkness and their reflections assembled in the safety glass.

There was a knock and Alastair the unit manager came in with his notes. He shut the door behind him by holding the latch down and slowly closing the door until it was seated in its frame and then releasing the latch very slowly until it clicked. Elizabeth turned to stare at him but he met eyes with no one and sat beyond Robin where he couldn't see her face.

Elizabeth laughed with a snort through her nose but if he heard it he did not acknowledge it. Andrew looked up idly, then back again to his notes. Time passed. Elizabeth checked three things in the notes and closed the folder again. Andrew picked up his phone and looked at it, and then he said, 'Well, would you like to summarise or shall I.'

He had stopped using her name.

Fire burns faster on slopes of certain angles, and it burns faster when the slope is enclosed on either side. This effect was unknown until 1987 when a small fire from a dropped cigarette burning under an old escalator in King's Cross station superheated 20 layers of the ceiling paint above. Paint that dated back to Queen Victoria. The flashover up into the ticket hall killed 31 people. It was called the trench effect. If the escalator had been shallower by 10 degrees it would have burned out.

'Oh, by all means,' said Elizabeth.

'A three-day history of increasingly severe abdominal pain,' said Andrew. 'She was seen by GP after hours at Adelaide Road.'

He told the story again and the surgeons flicked idly

through the notes.

One lax GP; on the third day another who was on the ball: anticipating surgery, he'd noted her last meal. Elizabeth corrected the blood pressure on arrival at ED by memory. Andrew named the ED nurses, noted that Richard was busy and ordered pain relief by phone.

'We'll skip the surgery here and circle back,' Andrew murmured and Elizabeth made a face of disbelief and checked the clock. It was 7:30 now and he had deliberately lied about the short meeting.

He noted Vladimir's post-surgery review of Lisa at midnight.

'Then, at 2 a.m. it was determined more invasive measures were needed, and cardiac arrest occurred during those measures and death was at 4:03 a.m. Is that right for everyone?'

'As I think I've made clear,' Elizabeth said, 'I visited Lisa at 11 p.m. The nurse on duty was assisting her with the CPAP mask. She wasn't liking it. I spoke to her. She spoke to me. I wished her well and left her there. I have no idea what they did to her. Why things went south as they did.'

'All right,' said Andrew. 'Let's now turn to the surgery.'

'Yes let's,' said Elizabeth, and her voice was strong.

'The notes from anaesthesia and your notes agree that anaesthesia commenced at 1:40 p.m. and surgery commenced at 1:50 p.m. You placed the camera port in Lisa via a sub-umbilical incision using the open Hasson technique.'

'That's correct.'

'The uh, camera and gas port was inserted into her abdomen and uh, insufflation commenced. Is that right, Robin, from your perspective in nursing?'

Robin looked up abruptly, then down at her notes. Elizabeth was looking away from her, directly at Jason Latham—a reach, a dare. He didn't even look up.

'Yes, that's correct,' said Robin.

'And Robin you say in your notes here that Mrs Taylor verbalised there was no gas?'

'Um,' Robin flicked through her notes. 'Um, yes, I've written here that at about 1:55 p.m. Liz, Mrs Taylor said that there was no gas flow.'

'What did she mean?' Andrew said. He sat back and put down the notes and the other surgeons laid down their notes and sat back.

'Um, I took it to mean that we had not achieved a safe pneumoperitoneum due to a lack of gas.'

'What's a safe pneumoperitoneum for those of us who are not generalists and don't know anything?'

'Um, that's a sufficient pressure of gas inside the abdomen that lifts the peritoneal sac away from internal structures that can be damaged by insertion of instruments. The um pressure of that would be a pressure of 10 millimetres mercury on the gas machine. Also it looks quite blown up.'

'A big belly.'

'That's right.'

'What happened then?'

Elizabeth breathed through her nose and Vladimir sat and stared at their reflections in the glass. Robin looked at them both and then at her notes.

'Um, she, Mrs Taylor, asked for a new gas bottle and Ms Chambers left theatre to get one.'

'That's Mei-Lynn Chambers?'

'Yes.'

'All right. Very good.'

'At that point I went to the gas tower and I saw that the gas hadn't been turned on properly.'

'And at that point the camera port had already been inserted using a 5-millimetre trocar and—'

Elizabeth interrupted. 'At that point we had visualisation of the abdominal cavity,' she said. 'We could see on the screens exactly what we were doing. We had about 8 millimetres of mercury pressure and—'

'I'm sorry Liz, can I just get Robin to fill us in from the perspective of nursing first of all before we come back round to you?'

Jason looked up at her.

'Of course,' she said. She smiled. 'Of course.'

'Yes, please, uh Robin, can you carry on?'

Andrew's tie was the old goldish one with paisley like ladybirds. The knot looked almost fossilised. The gap around his shirt neck was growing as he aged and shrank. Richard once told her that his father, who bought his clothes in London when he went to conferences, told him that the space between the rake of a shirt collar and the suit lapel was known in menswear as the credibility gap.

'Um—' Robin looked up at Elizabeth for a second and seemed to recede. 'Sorry what was the question?'

'Just carry on where you left off.'

'—Um, so. So I turned the gas back on.'

'Wait—so the gas bottle wasn't actually, in reality, empty?' Jason said. The room was quiet.

'No.'

'Oh. And what was the flow rate?' he said.

'It was about—I increased it but not beyond um six point five. That's the top it goes to.'

'Six point five, what would that be, Robin.'

'The gas tower measures flow rate in litres per minute. There's the flow rate and then there's the pressure you need to get to, and that's in millimetres of mercury.'

'So a flow speed and a destination. Like filling a petrol tank.'

'Yes.'

'And what was—'

'Hold on Jason,' Andrew said. 'What is the pressure required for a pneumoperitoneum again, Robin?'

'Ten millimetres mercury,' she said.

'Carry on Jason,' Andrew said to the notes.

Elizabeth was looking from one to the other smiling in disbelief but no one otherwise in the room looked at another person.

'And what was the pressure at that point?' Jason said. 'How much gas was actually in her abdomen? I mean, to be frank, was it safe to go sticking things in her?'

'Um, I don't know,' said Robin.

'You don't know,' said Jason. 'Is that right.'

'No, I don't know.'

'She cannot know,' said Vladimir.

The surgeons looked up.

'Sorry?'

Elizabeth breathed through her nose and seemed to relax.

'She cannot know,' Vladimir said. 'The indicator, indicator on the insufflator, this is gas tower, reads enough or not enough.'

He slowly, gently shrugged.

'It reads enough or not enough?'

'Yes.'

'For a trocar to be inserted?'

'Yes.'

'What do you mean?'

'Yes, or no. Go, don't go. Enough or not enough. There is

not a level.'

'So you can go ahead or you can't. A full tank. Green means go.'

Elizabeth sighed loudly.

'Yes.'

'So you actually can't know if you have some degree less pressure or what degree. Beneath 10, which you need to be safe. You can't know if you have 8 millimetres or some other number and decide to go on the basis of that.'

'No you cannot.' He shrugged again.

'You explicitly said there was 8 millimetres of pressure, Liz,' said Jason.

'There was direct visualisation of the organ space,' said Elizabeth. 'Excuse me, but at whatever actual pressure it was I could see and my clinical judgement was that there was sufficient pressure—'

'—to insert the next trocar?'

'That's right.'

'At the left iliac fossa.'

'No, I had already done that one before the problems with the gas,' Elizabeth said.

'So there were two'—Andrew flicked through the notes— 'two ports already inserted into Lisa.'

Elizabeth stared at him for using the name.

'That's correct, Andrew,' she said.

'By you.'

'Yes.'

'And then there were problems with the gas.'

'Yes.'

'And then the last trocar.'

'Yes.'

'Who inserted that last trocar, Liz,' said Andrew. Everyone

at the table but her own team looked up at her. 'Who put the last trocar in?'

Babies die in hot cars, left behind by tired parents in workplace carparks. It's called forgotten baby syndrome. In the US there were 677 children dead from vehicular heatstroke since 1998; 49 in 2010 alone. Roughly half were less than one year old. Average circumstances: 54 percent caused by child forgotten by caregiver. Only one survivor, in 2011, who suffered permanent brain damage. The father was convicted by a jury of misdemeanour child endangerment but the judge did not give him any jail time, because, he said, he had already sufficiently suffered. *Who measures this? What is sufficient?*

'I did.'

Robin looked up and over at her. Vladimir still didn't move. The entire table was silent. Vladimir seemed strangely pleased.

'You inserted the last trocar that caused the internal damage to this girl. Uh—' He leafed through the pages. 'A rent in the inferior vena cava. A cut in the posterior abdominal wall. A tear in the lumbar artery within the—'

'Yep.'

'Okay.'

'Look, it was slightly more complicated than that,' Elizabeth said. 'I remember it all clearly and completely. Under my instruction, Richard Whitehead—'

'Again I'd like to wonder aloud why in fact he is not here today,' said Jason.

'—I instructed Richard to insert the last trocar. I recall this completely and my team will corroborate this.'

'Hold on,' said Andrew.

'I am the team leader and I am the lead surgeon. I am the

leader. I instructed Richard to make the incision and to insert the trocar. I determined the timing.'

'Wait, *Richard* inserted the trocar?'

She could see herself in the reflection in the safety glass and she was straight-backed and good and she spoke to herself.

'Richard inserted the trocar on my instruction and it failed to penetrate. I told him to push harder.'

Andrew looked at Robin, at Vladimir.

'Told Richard.'

'That's right.'

'You instructed him to push harder.'

'I said give it some welly.'

'At that point, can I confirm, neither Richard nor you were aware of whether there was enough pressure—'

'I instructed my registrar for whom I am responsible to insert the last trocar and he did and at that point we noted internal bleeding on the screens and I called for instruments.'

'You decided to open.'

'We had to open.'

'Do you know what you're doing, Liz?'

'Yep.'

'Nursing?' said Andrew.

Robin's head snapped up as if from a dream. She looked from Andrew to Elizabeth in reflection, then down at her notes. 'Um—um. I, at that point I heard Mrs Taylor say mesenteric something. And then I heard her say quick we have to open.'

'Did Mrs Taylor instruct Richard to push the trocar harder?'

'Yes—'

'You converted to laparotomy. That's for you, Liz.'

'That's correct.'

'And you, Liz, you stemmed the bleeding and you sutured the cuts to the posterior abdominal wall, the IVC and the tear to the lumbar artery.'

'That's correct.'

'You performed those repairs?'

'That's correct, Andrew.'

'And it's your position that you are responsible for the insertion of the third trocar that caused the internal damage?'

'It was the sepsis that killed her, Andrew, and everybody here knows that.'

He looked at her and she looked back at him.

'It was my operation that caused that damage,' she said.

'That's your position.'

'Yes.'

'Thank you.'

They all sat very quietly for a time.

Elizabeth stared at her own reflection.

When she looked away she saw Robin watching her in the glass.

Smile on me.

And then Robin turned away.

The nose section had ripped away from

the payload bay cleanly, although a mass of electrical cables and umbilicals were torn from the cargo hold, fluttering behind the crew cabin as it shot through the thin air, still climbing.

Challenger's fuselage was suddenly open like a tube with its top off. Still flying at twice the speed of sound, the resulting rush of air that filled the payload bay overpressurized the structure and it broke apart from the inside out, disintegrating in flight. *Challenger*'s wings cartwheeled away on their own but the aft engine compartment held together, falling in one large piece toward the Atlantic Ocean, its engines on fire.

The TDRS satellite in *Challenger*'s cargo bay and its solid-fuel booster rocket were blown free as was the Spartan-Halley spacecraft. All this happened as the external tank gave up its load of propellant, which ignited in the atmosphere in what appeared to be an explosion. It was more of a sudden burning than an explosion. In any case, the two solid rockets emerged from the fireball of burning fuel and continued on, bereft of guidance from the shuttle's now-silent flight computers.

—*Challenger* disaster timeline

High winds aloft

She moved through the house, brushing her teeth. The wind outside blew. The house cracked in the pressure wave before the gust, as if it were tensing up. She stood in the doorway of the guest room that no one ever used, and continued brushing her teeth. She looked at the single bed and the chenille bedspread. A rosewood sideboard, and a bedside table by Arne Wahl Iversen. The room no one used. In the living room she stood in the middle of the thousand-dollar Afghan rug and brushed her teeth, looking at her bookshelves. Montaigne. Marcus Aurelius. Her epi textbooks, her textbooks. *Mason* by Rachel Barrowman. The flaw on the wall. On the facing wall the giant poster of a young Bruce Springsteen from *Nebraska*. The Bosch gas-electric cost her two and a half thousand dollars when she redid the kitchen and she'd only ever used the hob. On the bench sat the four dishes of their little dinner. She padded through to the patio, and her feet made sticking sounds on the boards. Outside a quarter moon up over the hockey stadium and clouds heading south. There were dead leaves in the chaise. White stains on the barbecue cover where standing water had pooled and dried undisturbed a thousand times since she bought it. Inside the toilet flushed. There was a snail on the brick and she flicked it into the garden with her toe and went back in. She locked the French doors and took down the Montaigne from the shelf. Robin was at the mirror in Elizabeth's pyjamas brushing her teeth and Elizabeth leaned past her to rinse her toothbrush and drop it in the Agee jamjar with the interdental brush she'd never used after the first time when it drew blood. The floorboards were cooler in the hallway. A bubbling grumble outside—a Satan's Slave on his big Harley opening up the throttle at the hill home to Berhampore. They called them Satan's Little Helpers. They were all old men now.

She climbed into her bed and sighed.

She could hear Robin's little ablutions, her neat spits. Hisses of brushing and pissing. The mysterious silences. Pad of her feet. She came in almost hunched, and closed the door quietly. Opened the right-hand wardrobe door to put her folded clothes on the shelf Elizabeth left clear for her clothes. Her toilet bag, her subsonic nursing Nikes. Robin climbed into bed. Diligent nurse, she was reading studies: checklist protocols and systematic reviews by some hot shit at Brigham and Women's, some astronaut from the VA.

Elizabeth inhaled sharply through her nose and breathed out again slowly.

Cicero, footnoted in the Montaigne: *As the scale of the balance must give way to the weight that presses it down, so the mind yields to demonstration.*

Silence. The house cracked. Then came the muffled roar. Elizabeth checked the alarm on her phone and put the phone on the nightstand and read on. Robin turned a page and the bed shifted as she scratched her calf with the toenails of her other foot. Smell of her handcream. The house cracked, and roared.

'Do you want lights out?' Robin whispered.

'No.'

The pōhutukawa rattled and scraped the roof. Muffled static. Vast, dark activity. Robin licked her fingertip and turned the page by dog-earing the top right corner and dragging it down across the printout. Hard on her books too. Spines white with lines where she cracks them open to lie beside her, to float flat upon cushions when she sits in the sun in yoga poses.

Elizabeth sighed.

'What time you up?' Robin said very quietly.

'Six.'

'Okay.'

'All right?'

'Yep for me.'

'Only got eggs.'

'That's good for me.'

Elizabeth closed her eyes and pushed her glasses up on her forehead and rubbed her nose where the pads left pale imprints in her skin that were almost permanent now. She opened her eyes and looked at the page of Montaigne, blurred and doubled.

'There's no more toast.'

'Yep. That's all right.'

'Butter. No toast.'

'Yep.'

'Useless.'

Robin reached out and put her hand on Elizabeth's thigh.

A second, even two, later than usual.

When Elizabeth woke the light was still on and Robin was turned away, breathing slow. Elizabeth had dreamed badly. Climbing through foul-smelling intestines that gave and gave beneath her. She got up, turned off the light and went and sat on the sofa in the living room in the dark.

At Mission Control they are observing

dozens of monitors, dozens of data sources. Initially they are as confused as the rest of those on the ground, looking up into the vast exhaust of the rockets.

At T+89.000 Jay Greene in mission control utters the first words since the explosion 13 seconds before, directed to the flight dynamics officer, known by the acronym FIDO:

'FIDO, trajectories . . .'

FIDO: 'Flight, filters got discreting sources. We're go.'

(*Filters* meant radar. *Discreting sources* meant that radar was now tracking multiple objects, in this case, fragments.)

Greene: 'Okay, all operators, watch your data carefully. Procedures, any help?'

Someone unknown: 'Negative, flight, no data.'

To the butcher's

The next day off with no on-call was Sunday. She woke early, read, washed all her things and hung them out in the garden. She reread the 1000 words of her response to the peer review and added a few here and there and went back to bed and masturbated. When she rose again she had eggs for lunch and lay on the chaise in the sun reading studies. When it was too hot she went inside and answered emails. Requests from agencies for consultations on capability building, requests to join expert advisory groups, and to co-author papers, requests for extensions, requests for revisions, requests for peer review.

And the phone was ringing.

'Elizabeth Taylor,' Elizabeth said.

'I think you mean Elizabeth Taylor, *bitch*.'

'Jessamine. How are you.'

'Excellent, excellent.'

'Oh, you're not.'

'What?'

'Oh Jess.'

'What?'

'You're scraping the last bits of a chocolate dairy food out of the tub with a teaspoon.'

'No I am not.'

'I can hear it. This is what you do when you call me.'

'I'm *not*.'

'You've stopped.'

'All right but I was finished before you said that anyway.'

'Well.'

'Weeeell. You're home.'

'Yeah. How did you know?'

'I called the hospital first.'

'Oh.'

'Yep.'

'What's up, Jess?'

'What's up. Well. I actually have a favour to ask you. That may well benefit us both.'

'Hmm?'

'Well. We were wondering if you might be interested in a little friend for a while. Well, not so little. But just a while.'

'Hmm?'

'So. Here's what it is. Peter and I've found a place in town and it's just no good for a big dog. It's an apartment just off Tory Street and there's just no way to make it work. It's too small and it's third floor in town. Really nice.'

Elizabeth held her breath and then breathed out through her nose.

'So—oh Jess.'

'No, it's just for a while. The house is on the market and there are open homes and he's working all the time and he just won't take him.'

'Stephen won't.'

'He won't. Point break. That's just the way he's gone.'

'Where are the kids?'

'They're with his parents. Peter's daughter Sarah is at his

mum's until we get the renovations done and we've organised her room.'

'So wait, she's moving in?'

'Yes. We'll share her with her mother. Which is fine.'

'I can't.'

'Atticus is really old, Liz. He'll be your friend. Totally house-trained. He just sits around in the sun all day and sleeps. Just a few weeks. He doesn't need anything. No needs. The occasional ear squeeze. A little jowl squeeze. I said *jowl*.'

'I am never home.'

'It doesn't matter. He's used to it. We're never home anyway.'

'Oh fucking hell Jess.'

'I knew it. I knew it. Thank you. *Thank you*. Just a couple of weeks.'

'Jess. Jess.'

'I—*love*—you.'

'I don't love you. I don't.'

She sat at her laptop with the draft of her response to the peer review until the light changed. There was no more food in the house and Robin wasn't coming over. She got her keys and went outside to take the Camry to the Island Bay Butchery for three lamb and mint sausages.

The sun was setting but it was still hot. She made a tight, fast U-turn and accelerated up the long slow hill and then she kept accelerating, pushed her foot down hard until the engine was on the very edge of a sound that could plausibly be blamed upon the slope, until she hit the flat by MacAlister Park and was driving at 90 kilometres an hour past the villas of the old people's home called Village at the Park.

She braked at the top of the rise and was back to 30 kilometres an hour the moment she crossed into the slow zone of Berhampore.

The lights stayed green and when she crossed the zebra crossing at the Romanian Church there was still no one around and she put her foot down hard again and the Camry seemed to hunch and gather itself and then it screamed as she did 80 past Wakefield Park into Island Bay and there was still no one on the roads and she was at 100 when she drove through the first Island Bay roundabout, ignoring the side streets, the Camry's tyres squealing on the ghost markings left behind by the new cycleway.

Down in Island Bay lived Mary Leonard, an anaesthetist, with her husband John, an English intensivist on the same team as Ben Matthews. Mary and John ran down Severn Street together, comparing their speeds by the radar speed signs that were everywhere now, that on Severn Street register runners if they can run fast enough. Mary and John had embroidered LIVE LOVE LAUGH cushions. Down here lived a retired professor of public health who taught her in Dunedin. Down here lived colleagues.

She turned left off the Parade up Tamar Street, crossing the edge of the cycleway, flattening the temporary plastic bollard and it hammered under the chassis as if far away.

Up the hill to the steep streets named after rivers.

Avon, Hudson, Volga, Thames.

She accelerated so hard the engine howled but the streets were so steep she was not breaking the speed limit.

A man mowing his lawn turned to look at just another silver station wagon passing by.

Hatchbacks, retaining walls, dead front lawns.

The valley opening up behind her.

Round the long corners the wheel slid in her palms, windows down, the cicadas screaming.

Under the clay cliffs of the top of Volga Street she was doing 90 kilometres an hour on the wrong side of the road and she glanced only once downhill before running the Give Way on and up Mt Albert Road without slowing down for the final climb towards Houghton Bay.

At the summit she pulled a 180 in the middle of the Buckley Road T without even looking but there was no one else looking either. And then she stopped.

Looking down at Wellington. All brown. A solitary bird on a wire. Smoke from the brush fires by the Tip Track in a red evening.

Why are you nothing to me? Why are you nothing compared to me?

She sat there for a time. Then she dropped the handbrake, stood on the pedal, rode the gears into third back down Mt Albert Road past Volga—the hardest corner because it was blind and a hairpin and there was a cliff. She was going too fast and crossed the centre line entirely to make it around but still there was no one coming. As she rounded the next corner onto the straightaway by the hockey fields she hugged the bank so close the wheels shuddered in the rough ground of the shoulder and tattered branches slapped and clawed at the windows on the passenger side.

All blind now, before the chicane that descended into Martin Luckie Park and the straightaway into Newtown. All blind on that corner but for one tiny window through the brush where she might catch a glimpse if someone was coming her way. There was nothing there unless there was a car too close and already inside the corner and she could not see them.

She breathed slowly out through her teeth.

I am the right one.

She lifted her foot from the brake and leaned her body into the door and the car dropped into the corner and she felt her stomach fall and the right front wheel lift from the asphalt.

Magpies wheeled over the park.

Villas with gingerbread trim and smug paint jobs.

The car shuddering and heaving.

There was no one.

She overcorrected on the left turn and the big car zigged and she corrected again and it zagged and then she was through. Straight onto Russell Terrace where she could see the red light above the hills over the hospital far away and where the warning sign did not read her speed but only SLOW DOWN and she slowed to maybe 70 before the Waripori Street stop sign, checking for reflections in the road signs or headlamps shining up the towers of the Mansfield Street estates and there were none and she took the chance and drove right through the intersection and only slowed down for the 40 zone at the Mansfield Road roundabout because after that there was a chance her car would be recognised, seen by someone from work.

Slowly through Newtown. Soft at the lights. Softly down Adelaide Road. Left-hand lane after the McDonald's into the centre lane by the Basin Reserve. Onto State Highway 1 after the Arras Tunnel, changing lanes. Picking up speed after the 70 zone by the cemetery and by the port and the siloes in scattered traffic she crossed three lanes at 170 kilometres per hour in one manoeuvre, breathing steadily, the clouds above her stupid and purple and bruised and moving over the water.

She drove out to Petone, circled the roundabout and came back in at exactly 100, breathing easy, ravenous now, following the limits all the way home. That night she slept outside on a rattan chaise in the garden, the warmth still rising from the brick of the patio, and if she dreamed she didn't remember and she woke at five, refreshed and ready for surgery.

Informed that day by paper letter the hospital had temporarily restricted her practice of laparoscopy and laparotomy in light of a public complaint and a history of comments by staff.

It is bitter—data

She lectured one afternoon a week in the Otago Medical School building, affixed to the hospital on Mein Street like a parasite. It was a guest lecture for a paper in the postgraduate diploma in public health. The students were a group of public health registrars, frustrated, ambitious pharmacists and the variously disappointed; idealists with jobs and children and not enough time, looking for a better way. In her briefcase she had pages of her handwritten data and two thumb drives.

Her presentation for PUBH 112 was on the individual clinical freedom of doctors to do as the evidence and their best instincts suggest. Versus guideline- and data-driven 'cookbook medicine'. The growing tensions between the two. At one point she asked them directly: Japanese hospitals don't use the same methods Toyota does. Why would you say that is? Later she descended to the basement floors of Wellington Hospital. In the elevator a young registrar from Auckland tried to ask her about an X-ray.

'Turn it the right way round, Susan,' she said.

The girl looked horrified and swapped it left for right. A stiff-limbed woman in a red gilet and jeans got on at 2, a patient, and Elizabeth looked at the registrar and the girl let the X-ray hang by her leg.

'Take it up with your consultant,' she said when the doors opened at B3. The girl just stood there in the lift after Elizabeth stepped out.

'It's Arthur,' she said.

'Please don't follow me.'

Down the corridor, ceiling tiles were still missing from the refurbishment. There were flat slabs of concrete visible through the holes. One fluorescent tube buzzed and went out. The door read Clinical Coding and inside was a pod of desks and an older man was slid back in his seat. A younger bearded man in the corner was bent forward almost lying on his keyboard. Several younger coders were about in the other desks and one had a huge coffee mug on which was printed 'Size Matters'. A limp poster on the wall read, 'To increase awareness and help promote clinical coding as a career option clinical coders are profiled on a widely publicised New Zealand Careers website. Also, a clinical coding brochure is available.'

'Hello,' she said, as she might have done to an unattended till in a department store.

The older man didn't budge. The younger ones didn't even look up. The bearded one turned and he had earbuds in she hadn't seen and she sighed.

He grasped his earbuds, sighed as well, and tugged them free.

'Hello?' he said.

She tapped her *#HelloMyNameIs* name tag with a fingertip. He leaned forward to read it. His neck was not shaven and he had hairy cheekbones.

'Oh, are you looking for quality and risk?'

'I'm looking for the clinical coding manager.'

'Yes?'

She looked around. The slumped older man hadn't moved.

'Is that you? Got five minutes for a chat?'

He'd almost shrunk in his chair and was looking all around him too.

'I'm sorry . . . ?' He peered at her name tag again.

'Liz Taylor. Mrs.'

She said it for him to hear. The tone. The 'Mrs'. She was a surgeon. This is dangerous ground.

'Oh. Sorry. Sorry. Yes? What can I do to help?' The coding manager exaggeratedly cast his eyes left and right and indicated a plastic-wrapped swivel chair. 'Pull up a pew.'

She looked at him for a long while and then looked down at the chair. She leaned down and she wiped it with the knife of her hand. She sat down and gave him her eyes.

'Now, I'm interested in the coding of mortality and 30-day complications rates for select surgical procedures,' she said. 'Specifically—'

'Ah ha ha,' he said, and grinned. 'Ha ha ha.' He leaned back in his chair and laced his hands behind his head. Stale striped green shirt with bastard cufflinks and pitstains under his arms. 'Ha ha. So. Yes. You're here about the minister's mistake. Just a few weeks to go now, isn't it. Before *publication* day.'

He was English, stale and stank of bachelor. Always the exhaustion, the contempt. The older patients looking behind her for the doctor. Calling her 'the lady doctor' once they got their heads around it. Sudden memory of Atelier, who called all the Filipina nurses Betty, wrist-deep in the vagina of a draped 26-year-old on the trolley when Elizabeth was about the same age. She could see his hand in the girl's abdomen, flexing inside her. His other hand gloved and waving like a conductor. *I do love me a good strong uterus*, the consultant said, grinning behind his mask.

She smiled another long moment. Raised her eyebrows for him.

'What do you mean, please?'

'This is public reporting isn't it?'

'I suppose it is.'

'Let foxes report goings-on in the henhouse. Bit short-sighted.'

He nodded and grinned and waited for her.

There was an urge, wasn't there, to just destroy him, and rebuild him in a more pleasing shape. In service. She could hear him tweaking his accent on the fly. Someone who hadn't lived up to his education. Or a bad marriage. Living in the minutiae out here. Living in miniature.

'I would like to learn more about how this is intended to be done at the coalface.'

'Ah ha.' He grinned. The sweat was dark in furrows between yellow corrugations of wild deodorant. This was his favourite shirt. He had one suit, a summer jacket and a tweed. She could see them hanging in darkness above a pile of old shoes. She hated him so much she could taste it like a Granny Smith apple.

'And I presume as clinical coding manager you know what you're talking about and how the ministry is planning to go ahead.'

'They've got everyone scrambling haven't they? Set the hares running down to coding to see everything's all right.'

'I don't have a lot of time as I'm sure you don't either.'

'Not the greatest level of foresight. Let's just apply a neo-liberal mindset to healthcare. Why not. Avedis Donabedian used to say doctors, nurses, they have a sacred cause.'

He was looking this way and that with his rehearsed disgust. 'Who?' she said.

She'd discovered the truth of a platitude in London, a platitude that was only more true at home. Whenever she was out of her depth or not to up to date she'd learned never to admit she did not know, had not read nor completely understood any given thing. To admit ignorance was not frank nor forthright and would not invite appreciation of her honesty. She'd learned instead to ask the smartest questions on the fly and ask them till she got her answers. To be eager. Drown them with eagerness. Say I want to understand. Please explain. No matter how much in London the answers came with a wet skim of satisfied disgust almost post-coital in its intimacy, she had her answers for next time. The knife in the ribs and the wallet in the pocket. In New Zealand it was different. In New Zealand they weren't so suspicious. They left you convinced you were as smart and charming as they had sounded to themselves. Not knowing they were bleeding out until they met you again later, in power.

'Explain their methodology, if you would, for me.'

'Oh.' He lowered his arms. 'Well. It's rank and spank. League tables. Name and shame.'

She stared at him.

'Publishing data by named surgeon to enable you and your fellow surgical colleagues to be ranked in the newspapers by your performance, isn't it? Nothing a journalist loves more than a bloodied-up surgeon. Bit of a class issue. Levels the playing field. And by performance we mean mortality and we mean the really serious complications. Death and infection and things going wrong. They intend to name you and shame you for what you've done.'

'I'd like to know a bit more of the technical detail'—she

looked around his desk for some sign of a name, found it—
'*David.*'

'Well, essentially, when we ping our data over to planning and funding, as we do monthly, Mrs Taylor, we're also sending over your individual surgeon rates and raw numbers for the ICD codes they're interested in. A select group of procedures. You're a general surgeon are you? Well you no doubt do a few of these procedures and they're counting up your mortality and complications. Death and disability for up to a month after the op. I'm guessing they've decided they have enough data and they'll dump rates and 95 percent confidence intervals for the performance of every single surgeon in the country on their website and call it job done. The *Herald* and the *Dom Post* and Mike Hosking and every armchair analyst is going to compare those rates, make a list and the first story in the morning will be the worst performing surgeon in the country is here at your local DHB and his name's now mud and his career both public and private is probably for all intents and purposes over.'

There were certain words where the way a person said them revealed the way they felt about them. Jew, was one. Gay. Black. Nurse. Mrs.

'You sound like you think it's bullshit.'

'Oh I'm all for it if it's done right.' He laughed. 'Do I think we were sold a pup? Yeah, well, perhaps. But once we survive the first storm we'll have everyone arguing the toss over worthy things like risk adjustment and case mix and a lot of people like you will be tramping down here—'

He was excited and losing control. She recognised the same rhythms in herself.

'—clutching their case notes asking us shouldn't the codes for this or that dead patient not be palliative rather than this myocardial infarct you've got marked here? Telling us they weren't doing anything interventional they were just easing the old girl out.'

'Uh huh?'

'Heard of Z51.5?'

'Sorry?'

'You will. The code for palliative care. No chemo, no scalpels, no more interventions, just morphine and flowers. A Z51.5 doesn't go on anyone's stats because they were already dying when they came in. Z51.5s went from 400 to 1800 a month inside five years once people realised the NHS was measuring. Everyone started going out quietly. I don't think secular trends quite explain a 350 percent jump.'

'Uh huh.'

'But ultimately once the bullshit and the bodies clear it's better for the patients.'

'Better for patients.'

'Yep.'

'And you know what's better for patients, do you. Sitting down here in front of your screens.'

He paused. Looked at her.

'Well, no offence but the colleges hide all this don't they? Retraining on the quiet. Patients never know anything went wrong. Staff learn to hide things. It's a bit of a closed shop, wouldn't you say. And why shouldn't a surgeon be held to the same standards as an Air New Zealand pilot?'

She gave him silence. He dropped his eyes.

'Of course we'd do it differently but what are we. We're just lowly coders for one DHB.'

'How would you do it then, David. And how does one get started, please.'

He looked up then. 'I'm sorry, are you *Elizabeth* Taylor?'

Standing in scrubs in the slowest queue in the world for Wishbone in the great atrium of the hospital concourse. Holding a pottle of muesli and yoghurt. Tapping the cellophane lid of the pottle with her fingers and pulsing on her feet. Sayzed Hussein, the neurosurgery consultant, passing her by with an Italian meatball wrap in his hand and gumboots on over his scrubs and he didn't give a shit. Didn't make eye contact and headed for the lifts. Elizabeth raised her eyebrows. *Fine, then.* The queue was staff and patients and families and it went right around the fridges. There were some DHB in suits at one of the tables. Two interns ahead of her. Tap tap tap, ta-tap tap tap. She sighed. The two interns were looking at one of their phones and they didn't stop or look up when they ordered their food. She waited for her coffee and the DHB men were looking at her. She gave them her eyes and they looked away. When she got her coffee she looked around for a table and saw the two interns were seated and looking at her, too.

Around her the hospital hummed. In the tiny office her hospital desk had nothing else on it but a phone, a hospital PC and a sharps box. The DHB had a news collation service called Spoonfeed that filtered content on words like healthcare, DHB, surgery, mental health. It sent out a daily email to all staff from the laundries to the boardroom with all domestic media stories to do with health.

The story five down from the top was from a website she didn't recognise. 'Angel of Death surgeon played death metal in botched op that killed our Lisa'. There were half a dozen blatant factual errors and five photographs threaded through the story. She came upon them as she scrolled down. The first was of the parents and the boyfriend, not the sister, she'd been spared, and the mother was holding a framed photograph of Lisa and they were sitting in a sofa in a picture window that looked out on a garden at their home. The next photo was a close-up of Lisa from the same framed photo. Then there were the two photographs of Elizabeth. One in black and white, cropped from the staff photo on the website, and the other was the one the father had taken. Ill-framed and blurry, she was in blue scrubs looking down at the camera and she had pale bags riddled with wrinkles beneath her eyes, wild, angry. The last photo was of her house. No one had forwarded her the story.

She'd been in one physical fight in her life in high school and the feeling was familiar. Another layer under the skin of her face. Racing heavily, wet and cold. Skin of her cheeks working, flinching, moving over it but it had no sensation and was distant and she had no control of how she looked. A giggly feeling, a light feeling. Girls in Rangi uniforms sneering. All the blue and tartan. Like a cage. So many cunts she couldn't beat them all. There in their midst, silent and watching her, her face pale, doing nothing: Jessica. It passed fairly quickly.

Patients under general call out and flail and dream and kick. They never know and no one tells them later. Theatre teams stand around and watch them with surprised smiles, waiting for their dreams to slow down, waiting for it to stop.

She closed the tab and she sat there.

Around her the hospital hummed.

Five minutes later she opened up the 125 KB Excel template from the thumb drive David had given her. The file was called 'cumulative_sum_failure_analysis.xlsb' and her heart beat lightly.

The Excel file had two workbooks. Named 'Personal' and 'National'.

She consulted the instructions David had written out for her on yellow Post-It notes.

The Personal Excel sheet had cells of data and a banal empty chart with x- and y-axes. Observed, expected, moving range. It represented change over time, with limits to show when mortality went out of control against an external standard. When complications were out of control.

She deleted the sample entries in the cells and entered her own mortality and complications data for a few years until the previous month.

She sneered at it and hit enter.

The chart assembled itself around her work.

She was a jagged blue line over time, leaping from zero, rising up from perfect, rising back to it. Beneath a ceiling of rose-red—the upper limit, the agreed standard. Then suddenly she leapt again, she was transcendent, she went higher, paused for breath, and higher, and she burst through.

Abruptly stopping as the data dried up.

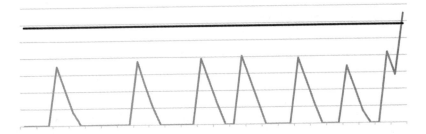

'Golf,' the coding manager had said. 'Golf. You finish your 18 holes and you have a score. One over par. Two under par.'

'I don't do golf,' she said. 'I'm not a lawyer.'

'Well okay, but you know how it works. There are 18 holes, 18 chances to play. Let's say those are your months of operations. At Bristol it was babies with malformed hearts. Switching arteries on the blue babies. Now at the end of your game you've got a score. How good were you? Pretty good. But did your game change? Did any holes go badly? Perhaps there was a group of them. Close together? How good are you really? When are you particularly good or particularly bad? Are you falling off and you don't know it? Imagine for every hole every shot over par is one dead baby more than the national average. You lose ten on the back nine you can make that up with the ten under par you saved on the front nine when you weren't tired. If they'd tracked them at Bristol using cusum they wouldn't have operated on Joshua Loveday. They'd have known and they wouldn't have killed him. They'd have known they were going wrong. It was originally used for munitions manufacture. Calibrations of shells. To check when the process was out of control.'

She sighed.

It wasn't that hard. Someone else had done the sums in the workbook template. She deleted the data with Lisa. Her blue line fell. The final few millimetres of blue disappeared and her deviations were within expected limits. She re-entered the data. She changed the name of the final month to Lisa. The blue line soared. It crossed the red, boundless and climbing, failing. She changed workbook from Personal to National. Deleted Richard and Lisa. Built the national chart, a funnel plot of general surgeons. The upper limit was in red and the lower limit was a friendly green and the limits narrowed and narrowed with numbers of cases, an eel trap from which she should never escape.

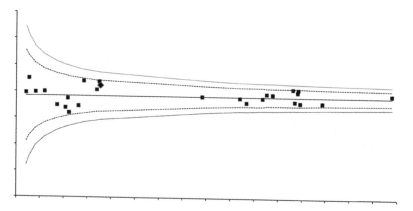

There she was, Elizabeth, a dot among dots. Every one a surgeon. Among her peers. Safe inside the funnel plot like a spider, *primus inter pares*. The expected limits of deaths for surgeons performing laparotomy. Her expected limits. Deaths on the y-axis, number of operations on the x. She was about halfway along the average number of procedures. She could do more. She added Richard, added Lisa.

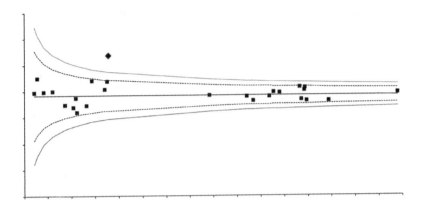

She had escaped the trap. Her dot was free of the limits. Free of all limits. She soared. Out there on her own. Out of control. Wrongly machined, wrongly calibrated. A wild munition tumbling in the sky. It was so quiet. *That thing in my face.* She deleted Lisa, and came back inside. She added her, and flew. Tumbling. She deleted Lisa, added her again. She did it a few more times.

Then she turned to work on her response to the peer review for Andrew.

She wrote for an hour. She cut and pasted her long response. She broke down every comment they had and added an asterisk after each comment and responded at length. The reviewer didn't like the *Lancet* paper. *Paragraph six on small numbers and identifying poor performers is simply wrong and ignores the seminal work of Marc de Leval and David Spiegelhalter in this area (now Sir David Spiegelhalter who examines risk for the NHS).* He had three references, all obscure and old. *Little evidence is produced to support these authors' facile conclusions.*

Don't give in. Double down. Always double down. She wrote and wrote. She restated the *Lancet* paper's finding.

Rolled her neck in her shoulders. Thanked the peer reviewers. And gutted them. *Thank you for this comment. However, we are keen to point out. Thank you for this comment which has helped us immensely in refining our argument. Thank you very much. We are grateful for this reviewer's comment. Thank you. However. Indeed, although. Despite these important points.* She anaesthetised them with praise and she gutted them thereafter. She did that work. It would fly or it wouldn't. She would fly or she wouldn't. It was an important paper. NZ was not the NHS. They didn't need to do this. They didn't need to do this. She wrote and wrote and wrote and then she suddenly sent it away to the *Royal London Journal*. She read the comments on the story about the surgery. Where people used her name. She opened the workbooks again. It was too late. Deleted Lisa. Entered her again. There she wasn't. There she was.

T+2 min 08 sec

Nesbitt: 'We have no downlink.'

The flaw

She woke at six, alone.

She lay there in the half dark. Then she got up and changed into gym gear, her thigh-long tights and a sports bra, and went into the living room. Atticus lay on the huge leather pouf Jessica had delivered with him. He watched her pass. Just his eyes. Wary, sad crescents of white below the dark brown irises.

Outside. Clean smell of the bush, and damp. A frighted blackbird rose from the barbecue, flared its wings and disappeared over the fence into the neighbour's backyard. She'd forgotten socks and she went back in and put on her work ones and took an apple as she came back through the kitchen.

Atticus lay and watched her.

Down the side of the house she stood in her sock feet on the dry concrete under the flax and ate the apple down and pitched the core up the back. She turned and crouched and unlocked the padlock and crawled in under the house and came back out in gumboots and overalls with the hammer and jimmy bar in one hand, and in the other a plastic Four Square bag with the Makita electric drill and drill bits along with five old unused borer bombs she'd found in the tool cabinet and then she went back inside the house.

In the living room she dragged the couch out from the north-facing wall. She unplugged the TV and router and the modem and dragged the chest on which the TV and electronics sat away from the wall too.

The flaw was at eye level. The previous owners had re-gibbed this wall and this wall only for some reason and the plasterboard was a decent job so she'd left it. But at eye level was the nub of a 5-millimetre bolt, sticking out just enough. The wall got no direct sun so the bolt cast no direct shadow. It was ignorable.

She laid down an old sheet as a drop cloth and laid the tools on it and put on her glasses and looked at the nub. It was sheared off at a slight angle and there was putty and paint around to smooth it off. She reached to it and she caressed it. Feeling the angle of the shear, where there might be purchase for the drill bit.

Then she picked up the hammer and she hit it as hard as she could.

The whole wall vibrated and the sash window rattled in the frame. Atticus laboured up from the leather pouf and walked out of the room with his head down and his tail between his legs.

She leaned in to examine the bolt. The paint had come off the end but it hadn't moved.

She guessed the size of the drill bit by eye and compared it to the nub. The chuck was tied with string to the trigger guard of the drill the way her father taught her, and she used it to screw the bit in tight and looked around for her ear muffs but she'd left them downstairs. She held the drill up high and straight and seated the tip against the nub of bolt and slowly squeezed the trigger. The drill hummed. She squeezed it tighter and the bit turned on the steel. She stopped and looked at the nub. It had made no impression. She squared her stance, raised her elbow, seated the bit and squeezed the trigger and leaned into it. The drill hummed, and the bit turned slowly then faster and then it slid off the bolt and punched through the gib. A neat hole. She tried again, adjusted her grip on the drill, leaning in. The drill hummed and the bit turned and then it jumped off the bolt again and through the plasterboard beside the first hole.

'Fucker,' she said aloud. She put the drill down and picked up the hammer and beat holes through the gib in a circle a rough metre around the bolt and then tore off the piece of gib hanging from the bolt nub and threw it behind her and stepped back.

It was a coach screw, 5-millimetre diameter galv steel sawed off as close to the wall as they could get their hacksaw, then filed down. It was impossible to know how deep in the tōtara stud. Not enough sticking out to get at it with the vice grips. She took up the hammer and bashed it a few more times and the windows rattled and clouds of borer dust rose in the room. It went no deeper. 'Why don't I use you as a fucking coathook,' she said. Then she rolled up the Afghan rug and pulled the TV and couch up against the south wall and smashed out the gib on the rest of the wall with the hammer and tore it down bare-handed and threw the pieces on the floor behind her as the room filled with dust. She went round with the jimmy bar snapping the heads off the thin gib screws and then she banged the sheared-off stubs into the timber with the hammer and more and more borer dust rose and then she went back to the bolt and looked at it.

She replaced the drill bit with a smaller diameter bit and

tightened it up with the chuck. She drilled 20 neat holes in the stud in a circle around the nub. The drill kicked and screamed when it hit the galv steel and she swore. Then she took up the hammer and bashed and bashed the bolt side to side and it barely moved so deep in the wood was it buried. She swung and hit and missed and dented the timber into shiny pits but the bolt was seated so deep she'd have to cut the stud through to the weatherboard to get it out and it was a load-bearing wall so she hit it and hit it and hit it and then she gave up.

She showered and walked down into Newtown at 6 p.m. for dinner at Monterey. She sat and ate curly fries and looked at her fingers and then finally turned on her phone. No one but Richard had texted her.

Hello Liz. I just wondered if we might have a chat please. Can I buy you a coffee or something?

At montrey, she replied. *U at hosp? Come over.*

He replied immediately.

She ate her burger. She ordered a ginger beer. He was there in ten minutes. Stood at the door in chinos and a polo shirt in Nantucket red. She raised her eyebrows for him and he came over and he sat and he examined the table.

'Thanks. Sorry to interrupt,' he said.

'You're not interrupting. What can we do for you, Richard?'

He took a breath and went to speak and didn't. There was something so generic about him. His good skin. Polo shirts and natural wool sweaters and woven belts. A sweet posh boy working overtime. Paddling hard underwater just to stay in place. The kindness in his tired eyes like a warning.

'I think it's ridiculous,' he said at last. 'Ridiculous and wrong.'

'What are we talking about that's specifically ridiculous today because I'm swamped in it,' she said.

He looked at her. It was safe to be appalled on her behalf and she didn't like it or trust it.

'That they've restricted you. *You*.'

'Well,' she said. She dropped a curly fry back in the basket. 'I'll work private till it sorts itself out. No shortage of work.'

'What does Alastair say?'

The waiter came then and he was a skinny 20-year-old and unknowably beautiful but still there was the air of decline and the threat of age that maybe was just the country and beautiful 20-year-old boys serving gourmet burgers. Richard looked down at the table and didn't look up when the waiter said, 'Hi guys, and how are we going here.'

Elizabeth smiled up at him and closed her eyes and shook her head. 'We're fine thanks.'

'Okay, just scream if you need me.'

'Yep.'

They waited till he was behind the counter.

'Alastair,' Elizabeth said towards the waiter far away, 'hasn't quite summoned up the sack yet.'

'Really? Nothing?' He shook his head at the table then he looked in her eyes. Hiding in his outrage. Performing for her.

'It's not how these things are done, Richard.'

'He *told* me it would be all right.'

'It will be.'

'But this is you.' He shook his head again. 'This is *you*.'

'You'll understand it. It will go to the College now. Watch it play out.' She looked past him. Assessing the clientele. She spoke very quietly and her face didn't change. He frowned and leaned in to hear her. 'You'll be all right. Just keep your head down and work. Don't start looking unlucky.'

He looked baffled, astonished. The restaurant seemed full of children. Anointed, some oil in their skin, in their hair, that placed them in a dream. Lisa's eyes over the CPAP mask, trying to breathe, in her dream, so late, so silver-blue, seeing Liz looking back, in her dream too. Rotorua girl, she wouldn't fit in here.

'We did the right thing, Richard,' she said to him. 'We did everything in our power inside and outside theatre. Mistakes may always happen.'

His eyes were twitching and red. She sat with her back straight and looked back at him.

What were the Williams family having for tea tonight?

'What does your father say?' she said.

He looked away over the restaurant, then back at her. 'I haven't told him anything yet.'

'Isn't that something you'd talk to him about anyway? You talk about work don't you?'

He winced, a sneer. 'Oh, I think he'd agree with you. Get on with it. And anyway, he's just been made head of surgery at Dunedin. So I'm not comfortable with what, you know, what position my telling him would sort of put him in.'

He shook his head at what he'd said, at what he meant, she couldn't tell.

'Oh?' she said.

He looked at her again. 'You didn't know? I assumed you knew all about the political stuff.'

'I'm suddenly finding myself a bit out of the loop.'

'You . . . I actually don't know what he'd say.'

'He'd probably say you're better than this.'

'Oh, probably. Maybe. I don't know if I am though.'

'Oh come on. Feeling that's part of it isn't it. How you get better.'

He eyed the waiters back behind the counter. His face swollen up, red around the eyes from the allergies.

'I'm—I'm actually having dreams about her,' he said.

There was a moment's pause she quickly sought to destroy.

'About the patient.'

'Yeah.'

'Oh. Well. Well, I'd say that's probably normal, isn't it? I'd say that's probably quite normal.'

'Not just her though.'

'Okay.'

'Other ones.'

'Right.'

'Sorry.'

'No.'

Elizabeth found herself looking away from him as his face worked. Ashamed for him, ashamed for being ashamed. For not being ready, not doing the required reading in time.

'Well,' she said. 'We should look into some ways of getting through it. Put together some coping strategies.' She could hear Atelier in her voice and hated him. 'Look, Richard, you're doing all right. This is normal.'

'Sort of scary dreams,' he laughed.

'They're just dreams.'

'Yep.'

'Would you be interested in, I mean, would you like some confidential counselling or something like that? I can speak to Alastair or go around him if you're not comfortable.'

He looked at the waiter and there was something new in his face when he looked back at her. There was a small silence and then he said, 'I know what you did for me. I just want you to know that I know what you've done for me.'

'Oh for God's sake,' she laughed. 'Don't be stupid. We'll talk more. Are you going to get something?'

He looked appalled.

'No.'

From the kitchen in a break in the music they could hear a cook talking.

'Dude if you fall over I might not catch you but I will help you up,' the voice said.

'Legit, I accept those terms,' a waitress said too quickly back at him.

They were all hopped up on hospo, maybe high, maybe just frazzled. Maybe this was just how they were. Elizabeth and Richard looked at each other, and Elizabeth tried a small smile. He looked at her, coldly, then he half imitated it and looked down at the table and there was a silence.

'Okay, well I've got to get going,' Elizabeth said. 'To be continued,' she said with false brightness.

He looked at her again and was unhidden.

Gauging what she had to get going.

Buried now, Lisa, anyway.

Going private

She rose at five, fed Atticus. Sat down with him. Scratched at the nubs behind his ears. He raised his head and then he lay down again, sighed, sad and heavy. She squeezed his ears and they were warm and she felt the fine leather inside, the fine hairs, the hint of wax greasy and clean on her fingertips. He sighed. She drank coffee and ate buttered toast on the rug beside him in his leather pouf, squeezing his ears, looking away from the skeleton of the stripped wall. Steam from her cup rising undisturbed in the silent room.

When she was dressed she went out and walked in the cool sunrise down a near-empty Adelaide Road to the private work. It was all clean and white and quiet in reception and the receptionist greeted her by name and gave her her credentials for the day. In the tearoom was a plastics surgeon she'd gone to med school with named Michael Garvin.

'Lizzy Loo!' he said and laughed loudly. 'How do you do.'

'Hi Michael.'

'My God, you've got fat!' he said. 'Look, you've got to come.'

'Hmm?'

'Here.'

He gave her a card. A birthday invitation. It read *Getting*

Fucking Old. Let's Get Fucking Old Together. Coco's Cantina &
126 Ponsonby Road.

'It's blow-out time Lizzy. This weekend. The *whole* weekend.
You must come. I'm on the seven o'clock up tonight.'

'What is this?'

'Degustation at Coco's then they've rented out an upstairs
studio on Ponsonby Road for two whole days. It's gonna be
mad. Peter Petrides' birthday bash. You know him from med
school don't you? He knows *you*. Ha ha ha. How are things?'

'Oh fine, fine. How's work.'

'So much. Oh, so much.' He leaned his head back and
closed his eyes and shook his head side to side moaning softly.
'So, so much.'

'Well.'

'And what's up with you?'

'Oh, working,' she said.

'Don't know why you do it. I mean the conditions. Look
around. Go private. Where everything's clean and quiet. Pay
off your mortgage.'

'I paid off my mortgage in 2007,' she said. 'What are you
on? Second marriage at 40? Worth it? You'll be sending your
complications down the road to us in due course I expect.'

'Ha ha ha. Yet here you are.'

'Yet here I am.'

Yet here she was, kissing Michael Garvin under a bush on
Orientation Week outside the Student Union in the rain 20
years ago. *Pashing* him, like they counted occasions, like it
was an outcome. *Pashing* occurred at whenever, no one knows
where. So drunk she didn't remember getting there or getting
back to the hall, just this memory of being there, under a huge
round bush on a circle of dry dirt a million miles through the
Dunedin rain from the noise and lights of the union as he

pashed her, as she pashed him. Sort of lovely, sheltered, lit by lights.

She found the bush sober a few days later the first week of classes and it was in the middle of the lawn outside the Union and it was a tiny round scrubby thing and the lawn wasn't very big either and everyone had seen and knew about it and it set the tone for a rep, a rep that took years to live down or rise into, complicate and make her own. She finally accidentally actually slept with Peter later, her neighbour at Selwyn and a sweetheart and soft, the night of the med school ball. Michael and a couple of med int students, one of whom was now head of orthopaedics at Canterbury, wrote REDRUM on the mirror in red lipstick and filled the room to the ceiling with screwed-up newspaper while they were passed out in bed together in there. Applause in the dining halls when they came in for breakfast late turned to stamping and chanting, *shame, shame, shame.* One of the private school med prats sang a few lines in Spanish about *amor perdido* in a passable tenor. Peter chose to bow and she gave them all the finger and the attention was a marker and she got better and better and better.

Later in the year Michael Garvin became the kind of guy who locked a D-lock from someone's bike round his neck and they lost the key and he paraded it around the hallways until his neck swelled up and he stopped laughing and got all grey and afraid and firemen had to cut it off with an angle grinder and no one hardly mentioned that again at all. He just got more successful. It felt sometimes that only the women and the gay men remember, the others put it behind their eyes and you could only see it later, certain lights, certain angles, certain conferences in Melbourne, certain specialties could see.

'Oh well, see you on the other side of your ulcer,' he said.

'I've got some tits to do.' He pointed to the card. 'Come. It's gonna be great.'

In pre-op Vladimir was gowning up.

'Oh hello, Vladi. Wasn't expecting to see you here,' she said. 'Who've we got.'

'Mmm.' He smiled, nodded left and right and they went over the charge sheet together.

'Is he consented yet?'

'Dr Smith is assisting. He is consenting the patient now.'

There was a silence between them. The nurses were unfamiliar apart from an Indian girl she'd seen before, couldn't remember her name. A new team of strangers. They were gowned up and prepping instruments. 'Hello everyone,' said Elizabeth.

'You remind me of a human error,' Vladimir said suddenly, and he smiled and waited.

'Oh?' said Elizabeth. She continued washing and said into the mirrors, 'Do go on, Vladi.'

Everyone laughed behind them. Vladimir was standing in the middle of the linoleum of pre-op, grinning, his hands already gloved.

'It is a story about a famous physicist called Albert Einstein,' he said. In his Irkutsk Russian he pronounced it *Eye-in-steen*.

'Who?' said Elizabeth rudely and looked sideways at him. '*Who*, Vladi?'

The senior nurse laughed and looked over at them.

'Eye-in-steen?' Vladi said, smiling. 'Eye in-steen.'

'Einstein,' said the Indian girl.

130

'Oh, Einstein, is it,' said Elizabeth and grinned at the senior nurse. 'All right. With you now.'

'Ah, Einstein,' said Vladimir, and smiled.

'Mm-hmm. What's your name again,' Elizabeth said, nodding to the Indian girl. 'You. What's your name?'

'Narysha,' she said.

'Okay.'

'Albert Einstein dies,' said Vladimir, 'and passes up into heaven. There he meets God, who is pleased with him. God says to Einstein, "You have done so well and for your reward, please, ask me anything."'

The phone rang and Narysha left to answer it. They were all variously paused, half-smiling, half-bored with his slow delivery, his telegraphed beats.

'Einstein says to God, "Okay God, I have a question. How did you create the universe and the stars and the forests and the blah blah blah?"'

Patiently they smiled for him. Vladimir made a face, a dutiful pout, of God.

'"Ah, well," God says. "I will show you." God goes to the whiteboard. And he begins to write equations.'

He sketched and wagged his hand and drew, did his God at the whiteboard. Then he stopped.

'But then Einstein says, "Hold on,"' Vladimir said. '"Yes, what is it?" God says. And Einstein says: "You made an error."'

Vladimir made a face of regret, and shrugged. Elizabeth started laughing ahead of the punchline.

'And God says, "I know. I . . . know."'

Vladimir watched them.

They all waited even as Elizabeth laughed and then they checked each other and then they laughed and then chuckled with him slightly longer then was necessary to be polite.

131

Elizabeth laughed loudly for them and then she stared at him but he was a stone.

Then he said, 'I will go fishing this weekend. Would you like to come?'

She frowned for him.

'Fishing?'

He shrugged. 'Fishing.'

'I don't *fish*, Vladi.'

He smiled. 'But you could try. You could learn.'

She just looked at him, half-smiling. He smiled back at her.

'Everything is always there. You go away from it,' he said. 'You take a rest. You come back.' And he smiled, and shrugged.

Narysha came back in.

'It's cancelled.'

'Oh come on,' Elizabeth said. 'What? Really?'

They all stood half-gowned and washed and looking at her.

'Yeah, I'm afraid so.'

'For fuck's sake, says who.'

'It's, I don't know. They just told me it's cancelled.'

'Well, Betty, find out who.'

Narysha went out again without replying and Vladimir slowly, gently shrugged again.

'What a waste of time,' Elizabeth said and no one looked at anyone else.

Elizabeth knocked at the door of the head of surgery and went straight in.

'Elizabeth,' said Mary and rose from her chair.

'Hi Mary.'

They kissed cheeks and stood at an angle to each other.

'Well, how are you?'

'Oh fine, fine. How's this position?'

'Oh, it's so good, Liz.' Mary rolled her eyes. '*So* good. *Such* a relief after DHB land. Have a seat. Tea?'

'I'm good. Fine.'

'Well, I'm sorry about this morning.' She smiled.

'What happened?'

'Oh you know. He ate something in the middle of the night and forgot about it and remembered all of a sudden during consent.'

'Oh.'

'Well. You're going through a bit over there I gather.'

'It's nothing. It'll blow over.'

'It's a cracked system, Liz.'

'Oh. Well, yes it is.'

'Between consent and the Health and Disability Commissioner who's just an ambulance at the bottom of the cliff all we've got is each other.'

'And family complaints.'

'And this new reporting system which who knows what *they'll* say.'

'They'll scream half of all surgeons are below average.'

'That's not funny, Liz.'

'No but there's the virtue of it being a fact. Anyway what we don't know is what the press will do with it.'

'Just ridiculous. It's unethical what they write.'

Elizabeth looked at her then. 'Look, how well known is this?'

'It's about, I can't lie.'

'Uh-huh.'

Mary smiled. 'But as you say it'll blow over. Look I'll be honest, most of the workload is orthopaedic at present anyway. There's a huge backlog of hips and knees. Spillover from public. They can't keep up. The numbers, Liz, are—' She shook her head, awestruck, moved and smiling, and laughed.

'Hmm.'

'I hear—I hear Robin's been moved.'

Elizabeth looked at her.

'To Hutt, yes.'

'Oh.'

They sat in silence. Out the window on the abandoned Tip Top bread factory by the Countdown there was graffiti that had reached the highest floor where there was seemingly nothing to grasp, nowhere to stand. The old sign still read *It's a Tip Top way of life*.

'Did he really eat something, Mary?' Elizabeth said.

Mary looked at her and smiled.

'That's what I'm told. Some spag bol from the fridge in the middle of the night. There's just nothing else we can use you for today. I'm so sorry to waste your time.'

Elizabeth smiled back.

Out into the sun. She checked her phone. There was nothing and it was half past nine and she walked home through emptied Newtown. Passing some of the frequent fliers who turn up at A&E limping along Riddiford Street. The gout. The bone spurs. The chronic obstructive pulmonary disease. The ankle broken for who knows how long and the old brown skin under the caked-on socks sloughing off in her hands. The impaired, limping, addicted, reeking of meths and smoking the butt, BO and sickly and goatish, trans-3-

methyl-2-hexenoic acid: the scent of schizophrenia. All of the plight and the damaged out after rush hour. Past Moon Bar, two mothers in big sunglasses with their young. The old wrecks outside the Newtown Bakery & Coffee Shoppe. The man in camouflage who always wears his bandanna and his reflective sunglasses even at night. The tall pale man with the tattooed skull who walks slowly, who likes camouflage too. After 9 a.m. all the Newtown unemployed out in the sun with her and the long day and the looping silences ahead.

She crossed to the shady side of the street by the McDonald's to take the alley up to Rintoul and on the traffic island she looked up at a sound.

In a break in the traffic came a young girl riding an old-fashioned bicycle with a basket, towing a boy on a skateboard behind her down the middle of the road.

They were maybe 20, 20-something. The girl serious and blond and pretty, leaning forward on her handlebars and frowning. The boy behind her young and cute and hairy and hanging on to some torn blanket tied around the seatpole. He was swerving to avoid the manhole covers. They were Lisa's age, really. Nothing to hide and nothing to lose and Elizabeth stopped dead on the traffic island and stood there like an idiot to watch them pass and leave her behind and cross the Constable Street intersection against the lights where they disappeared into the cars.

When she got home the house was sleepy and stuffy and hot. Baking in the sun all morning with the curtains open and the windows closed.

She went into the kitchen. She stood and stared at the skeleton of the stripped wall. The faint stench of the borer dust. She opened her laptop, booked a ticket on the 50-minute JetStar to Auckland mid-afternoon, shut it down. She put the laptop and the powerpack and her phone charger in a tote bag. She packed a single change of clothes into a carry-on suitcase and draped her navy cotton travel blazer over the extended handle and left it with the tote bag by the front door. *Certain errors by staff. Errors.* She went back to the kitchen. The borer bombs were sitting on the bench in the milky old Four Square bag. There were five. They looked like small paint tins and the brand on the faded paper labels read Borer Bomb. *Irregardless.* She opened the third drawer down and scraped around in the bottom through the string and the used-up Vivids and rubber bands and found some matches. *Yes, or no. Go, don't go. There is not a level.* At one point she said, 'You fucker,' out loud. She levered the cap off one of the bug bombs with a dinner knife and examined it. A powder like ash inside. She read the instructions on the side of the can. If there was an expiry date she couldn't find it. She lit the first one and it fizzed and made a hollow hiss and began to smoke immediately. *I'm not a toy. I'm not an employee.* She carried it over and put the lid down on the ground upside down and placed the bomb on the lid in front of the stripped wall. *I am the team leader. I save them with my skills. With all I am and have become.* A stinging white gas, clean like steam yet opaque, that rose quickly and did not thin. She held her breath and went to the French doors at the back to check the lock and the deadbolt, then she took the bag of bombs and the dinner knife and the matches into the hall. *I am the lead surgeon. I'm God, I'm fate.* She lit one there, and one in the bathroom, which was the wrong way around as she had to step through the smoke over the one in the hall to get to her bedroom. *I'll rise above you. Burst you.* She lit one of the bombs at the door and she slid it across the smooth, polyurethaned kauri to the foot of the bed, and pulled the door to. She lit the last one in the middle of the guest room and the house was fairly full of the insecticide already when she took up her blazer, her suitcase and the tote, shut the front door on it all, and headed down to Riddiford to find a taxi to take her to the airport.

At about 73 seconds in, the solid rocket

boosters emerge from the fireball and corkscrew wildly high into the atmosphere out of control. The shuttle itself is pushed sideways at Mach 2 into G-forces at an angle it was not designed to withstand. It breaks into several parts. The tail and engines fall on fire. The nose and reinforced crew cabin with the seven astronauts inside continues to climb, a further 5 kilometres into the sky, before it peaks. The cabin is found later on camera, a tiny white cube falling across a contrail.

It falls to the ocean for two minutes and 45 seconds, long enough for three astronauts to open the lever locks and activate the switches for emergency air packs as the cabin slowly decompresses.

Nature cannot be fooled

She bought some shoes and a little black silk dress with a deep décolletage off the rack at Karen Walker on Ponsonby Road. In the Airbnb on O'Neill Street she charged her phone and drank two whiskies as she showered and dressed and did her make-up. Then she went out in the warm Auckland night with a clutch in which there was nothing else but her phone, $500 in $100 notes and two cards: credit and birthday.

The shoes were killing her by Hepburn Street and she took them off and walked barefoot on the grass of Western Park but had to put them back on when she ran out of park after Hopetoun Street and by the time she got to the end of K Road she was hobbling.

She flagged down a taxi at the Mobil and the driver was an Iraqi with a crucifix hanging from his rearview.

'Coco's, just down K Road.'

'Too short.'

'Sorry?'

'Too short.' He shrugged. 'Too short distance.'

She opened the clasp and pulled out a hundred dollar bill and dropped it on the passenger seat beside him and he looked at her in the rearview and picked it up and put the car into drive and as they drove the 400 metres down K Road and across the motorway she stared out at the skeletons of the high rises going up above Freemans Bay and the chains from the cranes above them swaying in the warm winds off the Gulf.

She ran barefoot through the traffic across K Road and Renee herself, one of the owners, was serving at the tables out front.

'Oh hello,' Elizabeth said, smiling and smiling, 'I'm looking for Peter Petrides' function, if you don't mind.'

The woman looked at her briefly and at her feet and said, 'It's upstairs but there is a limit on numbers for the kitchen, I'm afraid.'

'Oh, I'm not eating,' Elizabeth said, and smiled and smiled.

The Mana Room upstairs was close and hot and not nearly big enough. The surgeons were seated and halfway through their meal and already drunk and she was late. Michael Garvin was sitting at the far end and she had to squeeze past them all, all the ones she didn't know, to get to him, who she didn't know either, between the wall and the backs of their chairs and she didn't introduce herself or say excuse me to any of them.

The man beside Michael looked up at her as she squeezed past and he said, as if it was funny but also horribly dank, 'Oh just feel your way through.' Michael was sitting next to a Chinese woman in her 30s who was leaning on him. He looked up, bleary and red-faced and happy. His smile just barely changed when he saw her.

'Oh Lizzy Loo. You came.'

'Michael,' she said, and she leaned down and kissed him on the lips a second too long.

'Oh,' he said. 'Yes. Liz Taylor everyone. Everyone, Liz.' He flapped his hands disinterestedly down the table but they'd lost interest too.

She stood there beside him a moment. 'So, where's Peter?' she said.

Michael looked slowly around.

'I don't actually know. Little boy's room?' he said. They'd all turned away.

She stood there.

'Oh,' he said, after a beat. 'Right. Budge up, budge up.' He wobbled side to side and pulled his chair beneath him with both hands. 'I think there are more chairs in the corner.' She stood there, the whisky hot in her cheeks. The Chinese woman sat up straighter away from him, smiling with her lips closed. 'Oh, right, look,' he said. 'Right, pass us down a chair please. A chair please.' It was all ruined already as she stood in the narrow gap between the back of his chair and the wall and the surgeons shuffled their chairs together to make a space and a chair was passed hand to hand over the table and forced into the gap and she had to lift it out to fit in front of it but couldn't so she had to climb onto it and then sit down and tuck her legs under the table and the surgeons looked at her and then at their companions.

'How are things?' she said and reached across the table for a bottle of red wine.

'Oh fine, fine. I didn't think you'd make it with all that work on. Look I don't think we've got enough glasses, do we.'

'Oh, this is fine,' she said and she poured the wine into a tumbler but it had an inch of water inside already.

'Oh, a rosé,' the woman said and they laughed and

Elizabeth did too and she drank a sip and then a gulp and she said, 'Lovely, too, actually,' and laughed horribly at her and the woman smiled horribly back for her.

'Are you in plastics as well?' Elizabeth said brightly. 'Private I suppose?'

'That's right,' the woman said.

'Liz is a general surgeon at Wellington,' Michael said. 'She's basically a charitable institution. Mostly public, anyway, isn't that right, Liz?' He smiled and drank his wine. 'Don't know how she does it. Why, rather, ha ha.'

The woman was thin, rich, perfect. Her smile had gone and she raised her eyebrows. Elizabeth stared at her.

'I don't suppose you can be too happy with this big data release, are you?' the woman smiled as she asked and then stopped.

Elizabeth raised her glass. 'Oh,' she said, 'well,' and she drank it down and refilled it and they watched her do it, the glass and the bottle in her hands.

'What's that then?' Michael said.

'The Ministry of Health is publishing surgical data or something,' the woman said. 'Aren't there privacy issues?'

'Yes,' said Michael, laughing. 'What about our right to privacy?'

'It's a lot of fucking bullshit,' Elizabeth said.

There was a silence and Michael laughed again.

'Well,' said the woman.

A waiter came in from the door to the stairs carrying two huge stainless steel sharing platters.

'Doesn't affect us and frankly don't know why you put up with it,' Michael said, watching the food. 'Look, Liz, we might be able to sneak you a few bites but I don't think you're in on the meal, is that all right?'

She smiled again for him. 'I'm not a dog, Michael,' she said and laughed and there were a few of them checking her now. 'I've eaten thanks. Anyway, it doesn't affect me. I'm on CME sabbatical right now.'

Michael frowned, half-smiled.

'You're on *sabbatical* now are you?' he said. 'You *seem* kind of hungry.' They moved the glass and the bottle for the waiter to lay the platter out and Elizabeth topped up her glass and then she refilled Michael's and the woman's. 'And angry. Which is good for pace bowlers but I don't know about surgery,' he said. 'Um, actually mine was the Bordeaux but never mind.'

'Bit of spag bol is this?' Elizabeth said. 'Sorry, what was your name?'

'Oh sorry, this is Hilary,' Michael said.

'Oh.'

'Yes.'

'Hi.'

'Okay.'

And then they sat silently looking away from each other at the other surgeons who were talking happily as they served their food to one another and ate their food and Elizabeth filled her glass again and poured the last few drops from the bottle into Michael's glass and he sighed and watched her as she drank her wine and she reached down the table for a new bottle and then her phone rang.

It was Richard. She tapped Ignore with Message and chose *I can't talk right now* and then took a long time typing *sorry I'm at a dinner everything all right.*

'Here he is,' Michael said. 'Peter. Peter, look who came.' Peter Petrides was at the door. He was wearing a toga and she hadn't seen him since medical school and he'd gotten fat and

143

creamy and clearly didn't recognise her.

She stood up quickly with her phone in her hand and her other hand over the mouthpiece and she said, 'Sorry, I've got to take this, see you at the thing after dinner?' and Michael shrugged and looked confused and laughed and she pushed her chair back crookedly up against the wall and climbed over it and squeezed sideways past all the chairs again and the surgeons looked up at her passing and ooched themselves closer in to the table to let her out and as she passed Peter she held the phone to her ear and she nodded and pointed at it and he just looked bewildered.

She was at the door before he stopped her. She turned with the dead phone to her ear and he stood there smiling, and shrugged and made a sad face for her. Then he mouthed, *It's me birthday.*

Elizabeth looked coldly at him. The phone to her ear. She blinked, and then she said, 'Uh, hold on,' and it was weird and half to the phone and half to him. She turned away from him and looked at the screen. *No bother*, Richard had written. She turned it off, turned back.

'Hi Peter,' she said.

'Lizzy,' he said. 'Give us a hug then? On me birthday?'

'Oh for God's sake,' she said, and then he laughed, and she laughed too, and she hugged him. He held her back and looked at her with faux shock.

'Are you *off*? I mean, *come* on.'

'Yeah well. Few things to do in town.'

'You all right? Haven't seen you in an age.'

'Yep, I'm pretty good. You?'

'Oh well,' he said, and he smiled limply. 'You look ravishing.'

'Wish I could say the same,' she said.

'This, Liz,' he gestured at the toga, 'is bespoke.'

144

They looked at each other fairly frankly for a long time. Then he said, 'Are you really off?'

'Yep.'

'*No.*'

'Got to.'

'Come along to the thing after?'

'Oh, maybe.'

'Go on. Go *on.* So much to talk about. How *are* you?'

'Oh, you know. Work.'

He nodded then and he was still and watched her and she saw the doctor in him again.

'You've made quite the name for yourself, haven't you?' he said. 'It's good. Wish I could say I wasn't envious. It's ruined me up here.'

She checked his face, how he held his hands. *Was he being sarcastic?*

'How do you mean?' she said, entirely mined of intonation.

'There were a few bright stars, I mean they were all *brilliant*, but you were so the best. You just always made it so hard for yourself.'

'Uh huh? Been doing a bit of analysis have you. You've got no idea.'

'See?' he said. 'See?' He laughed and made himself look hurt. 'Can't actually take a compliment. The greatest self-saboteur of them all. Anyway. You *look* great.'

'So do you Peter,' she tried.

'Oh, I know *that*,' he said. 'God, remember that central line you put in and you refused to do it unless everyone got out of the sterile field and you were like citing all these absurd rules from some CDC warning from the 80s. And 15 years later it's a bundle and everyone has to do it. God that was good. Well I hope you'll remember us when you're head of surgery. Bit late for me now.'

He sighed, did his theatre. They were doing what they did at university.

'Oh, poor Peter,' she said. 'Poor, poor Peter.' Some of the other surgeons were watching them now. He laughed, and he said, 'I just need a nuggle, on me birthday.'

She sighed for him, shook her head. And then she gave him a nuggle, his cuddle and hug, and he sighed and rested on her.

'Ahhh,' he said.

'Mmm hmm.'

'Signalling it's over,' he said.

'Mm-hm.'

He straightened and smiled. All weak and rich.

'Seriously, do come. I'd love to hear how things are going. People just say how brilliant you are. How *good* you are.'

She made a grumpy face, half looked away.

'Oh well, I'll see.'

'See, go on.'

'I'll see.'

'Go on.'

She walked barefoot down K Road with the shoes dangling from one hand. She crossed to a pub called the Thirsty Dog and inside they were playing 'Crimson and Clover' by Tommy James and the Shondells and the Shondells sang,

Now I don't hardly know her,

but I think I could love her

She stood at the bar and ordered a single malt no ice no

146

water and she downloaded Excel from the App Store and tried to get it to work on her iPhone but it had limited functionality unless you logged in with Office 365 and it only loaded the worksheet but not the graph and it was just cells and cells of her data and didn't look like anything much damning.

Yeah, my mind's such a sweet thing

I wanna do everything

And the song played the chorus over and over and then it changed key and did it again and she stared at herself in the mirror behind the bar and almost cried and smirked bravely and drank her whisky and ordered another and the soft warm Auckland breezes washed in the open doors to the bar and there was cricket on the TV.

Crimson and clover, over and over . . .

And then she remembered Atticus.

Cumulative sum of failure

Lying in the hallway was one of her surgeon's caps, the one with the print of a brain on it. Some of her clothes were strewn down the hall, and there was a fine white residue over everything. A dusty, ammoniac smell. The door made a hush sound as she opened it because behind the door were more of her clothes, all ripped up. The white paint on the inside of the door up to the latch was clawed through to the timber. It was incredibly quiet. There were paw prints in the dust in a path up and down the hallway, thousands of paw prints, and they circled the blackened tin in the middle of the hall by the bathroom and went into the living room.

In the living room everything was coated in white. The couch cushions were pulled awry and the path of prints went through the room in a semi-circle around the bomb by the stripped wall. The paw prints led through the kitchen to the French doors. The glass was grey and streaked with dried spittle and claw marks as high as the latch and the wood was torn at the lower sill and there was some blood and scuffmarks in a patch on the tile.

In the bathroom the floor was covered in toiletries. The white dust coated everything but the bottom of the stained glass window over the vanity. It was smeared grey with dried spittle and in the sink there were claw marks and hairs on the porcelain where he had climbed up to get to the window and fallen down.

Her bedroom door was open and the wardrobe doors had been opened too. There were claw marks on the wood. The ceramics from the window sill were smashed on the ground and there were books and papers strewn everywhere and there was spit and smeared dust on the window. Paw prints in the pale dust led in a path through the door and around the tin to Robin's side of the bed and back around to her side of the bed and back out through the door and there were ripped pieces of her clothes strewn everywhere and in the centre of the bed was his shape under the duvet.

Cumulative sum of failure 2

She carried him to the car wrapped in the duvet and laid him in the back seat and drove him to the SPCA in the old fever hospital in Alexandra Park and they told her it was the wrong place and told her where to go. She carried him back out and put him back in the car and drove to the after-hours clinic in Ngauranga Gorge and carried the heavy dog into reception and a young vet led her into a surgery. She explained what she'd done and how she'd found him and showed him the borer bomb tin she'd brought. The vet looked at her and listened carefully and then carefully unwrapped him. His fur was matted with the grey dust and there was foam and black blood on his muzzle and the pads of his paws were ripped and his eyes swollen closed.

The vet hardly spoke to her and examined the body briefly and then asked if she would like him cremated and she cried and cried and then pulled herself together and explained that the dog wasn't hers and after a while the vet put his arm around her and then he took it away again.

'He would've gone there to die because it smelled like you, though,' the vet said into the silence. 'It's why they rip up the stuff and spread it round them? So they feel surrounded by you.'

Cumulative sum of failure 3

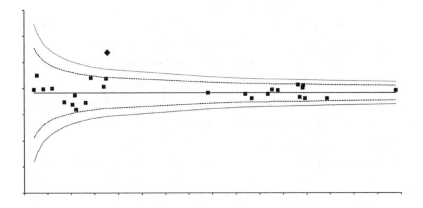

Who was watching, in that silence?

Crowds in Florida from the grandstands at Kennedy Space Center, a few miles from Pad B, Launch Complex 39, where *Challenger* is to rise. Space shuttle launches in 1986 were routine and *Challenger* is not broadcast live on the big TV channels. The crowds are mostly enthusiasts, family. Many are older. Wearing sunglasses and scarves, holding binoculars and cameras with telephoto lenses. Peering up. Astronaut Christa McAuliffe's parents are there, and students from the school where she taught. The first teacher in space. They go quiet, and they look around at others about them.

Silent home video emerges years later, filmed from Florida suburbs. The distorted VHS shows only a line of roofs, a near-perpendicular line of white in an empty sky on some ultimate incidence, bursting, splaying into two, going out.

At 76.4 seconds into flight the wild right solid rocket booster automatically releases its drogue and parachute which is immediately consumed by its own fire. At 110 seconds the range master fires the self-destruct charges on both SRBs as they roam freely through the Atlantic sky. The small explosions clearly visible on camera later. Blackfaced poppies fringed in white, blooming briefly off the side of the white light and smoke of the wake of the SRBs viewed from Earth. Both rockets go out instantly.

Publication day

She tied her hair back hard in a bun and took her time over it, then she did her make-up. Then she walked to the hospital in the dawn, clear and cool, and nothing but the cafés were open and she crossed the road by Newtown School.

On the third floor in the nurses' booth were only Mei-Lynn and a Filipina locum nurse Elizabeth didn't know.

'Good morning,' Elizabeth said brightly at the door and looked around, actorly, for a computer. 'I'm going to work in here for a bit if that's all right.'

Mei-Lynn didn't say anything. The Filipina woman said, 'Good morning, Doctor,' and was oblivious. Mei-Lynn quickly gathered some papers and left straight away. There was a moment's quiet and then Elizabeth sat down at the PC in the corner.

'Where's Richard today?' she asked.

The Filipina nurse looked up. 'I think he is off sick again. He wasn't in yesterday.'

'Oh?'

She got down to work. Among dozens of emails unanswered for days now was a recent one from a D. Cohen with the subject 'Your submission'.

They had rejected the manuscript in that gruff way they did.

Dear Drs Taylor and McGrath.

We are sorry but we cannot accept your manuscript in its present form. The Royal London Journal of Medicine publishes only 3% of the papers submitted each year and we regret that we cannot give a personalised response to each submission.

Etc. and etc.

And then after the boilerplate was a message from an actual person.

Hi, though not keen on the actual paper we enjoyed the response to the peer reviewers. Timely and a good tone.

We wonder if you would consider revising and resubmitting as an editorial on the New Zealand experience of releasing data? It will depend how fast you can get the proof back to us, but given this is happening right now, and the recent open letter on this issue in the Guardian *by the Royal College of Surgeons calling for our own scheme to be abandoned, we're thinking vaguely about the cover.*

Cheers, Denise.

Denise Cohen, fellow in surgery at Cambridge then *Royal London* views editor for 20 years, 50,000 followers on Twitter and she'd written a book. Written as if everyone knew who she was and everyone did.

The hospital hummed around her, and people passed behind the glass. She got to work. This close to publication she could change it now or never. Keep what worked. Perform the least manoeuvre. Polish and publish and perish and be damned. She edited and annotated and rewrote. It was easy to be uncertain and it was good to work.

At the top of the proof it read TITLE TK and a bubbled comment read *Suggestions?* Underneath it: *Elizabeth Taylor.*

Surgeon? Wellington Hospital, Wellington, New Zealand. Andrew McGrath. Head of surgery? Wellington as well?

Nurses came and went. A locum surgeon she didn't know looked in, around, and left again. Alastair passed down the hallway looking straight ahead. He clearly saw her, clearly looked away again down the corridor and was suddenly gone. She wrote, she edited, she added bubbled comments. The hospital hummed, it persisted. Around 8 a.m. the ward was alive and the anaesthesiologist and theatre coordinator for the day was standing half in and half out of the door with a clipboard. Susan Jones, the registrar from Auckland, approached him. A smile all ready. Elizabeth watched her. Susan made a nuzzling gesture with her head, smiling. Sidled up to him. He was a 30-year-old man with a fixed grin and a tattooed arm and sensing her he made a serious face without looking up, and he said, 'Heeeere's trouble.'

Susan mimed a shocked face and put her hands to her breast and made wide eyes for him and said, '*No.*' She looked from side to side. 'Me? I'm not trouble.'

'Oh yes you are. You're trouble. I know all about you,' he said, and he changed his face to a smile and laughed in sucking slurps in his cheeks. 'You're trouble. What do you want you naughty wee girl.'

'Well I was just *wondering . . .*' she said. She was casting her eyes over the ceiling and then her face became a great smiling wince as if she were watching something terrible occur. '. . . I was just *wondering* if we could just possibly fit Mr Pattinson in late this morning. I know. I *know.*'

He became very serious and looked down at the clipboard. He frowned at it and squinted. Then he moved the clipboard and looked at her up and down, slowly from her feet to her face and back again, twice. Then he raised the clipboard again and looked at it and then he frowned and then he sighed.

'You want to fit Mr Pattinson in last minute, do you.'

'If we could. I'm so sorry.'

'Slip him in when you feel like it.'

Susan laughed, almost gasping, her face moving, her eyes almost closed.

Elizabeth typed and edited and read. All the arguments lined up against what was now accomplished.

'Just slip him in. No heads up. No phone call. No glass of wine, no small talk, no foreplay or anything,' he said, shaking his head. 'Not even a kiss.'

Susan looked for a moment slightly lost and kept her smile. She said, 'Yep, if you could. We really need that bed for tomorrow and it would be *so* nice.'

'It'll hurt. It'll *sting*,' the theatre coordinator said to the clipboard. 'Feel sorry for the man.'

'Oh thank you *so* much,' Susan said. 'That's awesome. Thanks *so* much.'

'Well you're pretty desperate, I'll see what I can do, hold on,' he said and he'd taken his phone from his pocket and he turned away down the hall to answer it.

Elizabeth typed, and edited. Deleted and restored.

When he was gone Susan took out her phone and stood still. The booth was otherwise empty. She typed on her phone and all expression had gone from her face. Then she went and sat at a computer and typed.

Elizabeth finished the proof. She uploaded it to the manuscript manager and added a short cover letter addressed to Denise Cohen. Thanking the *Royal London Journal of Medicine* for this opportunity, referring to her by name.

Elizabeth gathered up her papers and journals and put them in her tote bag and stood up.

She looked at the back of Susan's head.

'You don't have to do that, you know,' Elizabeth said.

The woman swung around in her seat. 'Excuse me?' she said. 'Do what?'

'You don't have to do that.'

The woman looked angry but moved behind her eyes. She looked away from Elizabeth. Then she raised her eyebrows and looked directly at Elizabeth and was about to speak but then something seemed to overwhelm her and she didn't.

Elizabeth was halfway home when she received an email from Andrew.

The astronauts

She knocked on the door and waited.

'Come,' his voice finally said.

He was in his grey suit. The double-breasted with the peak lapels. He sat at his desk writing. He looked up and beckoned her without smiling and bent again to his work.

She sat.

He signed the document and sat back slightly.

'Hello Liz.'

'Hi Andrew.'

'Well, look I have some bad news.'

'Oh?' She raised her eyebrows for him.

'Look, Richard Whitehead has killed himself.'

She blinked. His office always seemed larger inside than was possible from the layout of the corridor. A glossy plant had dust on its leaves in the corner. Diplomas everywhere.

'What,' she said with no inflection.

'I'm afraid so.'

There was a silence and he watched her.

'Well that silly bugger,' she said. 'That stupid bugger.'

'Ah,' he said. He sighed. 'Yes.' He watched her. Then he moved his eyes away over the office as her face worked.

At last she said, 'When did this happen.'

'I don't really have any details, I'm afraid. I think family or a girlfriend found him. Staff don't know at present. Do you want to know the circumstances?'

'Yes.'

'It was a hanging at home in a garage and this occurred yesterday. That's all I'm aware of.'

'That stupid bugger.'

He watched her. He said, 'Do you have this in hand?'

'Yes,' she said, after a moment. 'Yes, I do.'

'This is a very bad business and a very poor show for the hospital and this department and we need to put a stop to all gossip and speculation and uncertainty before it starts. It is down to us to control this situation.'

She breathed in through her nose and out through her nose.

'Does his father know?'

'Yes, yes. Brian has flown up and will shortly be giving a statement to the media and is handling the funeral tomorrow. It's to be family only. Richard's body is being held in the hospital morgue.'

'Okay. What—what can I do?'

'It is family only.'

'I understand that.'

'I assume you probably have some thoughts as to what this is about.'

'I think I probably do.'

'It's not an uncommon phenomenon. Burnout. I suspect this will be a first for a lot of staff here, however, and we need a united front. Let's have one version of the truth, as it were, for the sake of everyone.'

'How exactly do you mean?'

'Let's be very clear. I wasn't sure which way any of this would go. This was a very tricky situation from an administrative point of view. Here we have you. You're an F-16, Elizabeth. You're fast, you're effective and you represent a considerable investment of institutional resources. You are valuable. But you're not cut from marble and I think we've observed that in the last little while.'

She stared at him.

'My father,' he said, 'was a surgeon in Korea. He was a prisoner of war and he told me how he took the limb traumas in the camps for walks down the latrines to conduct his examinations. For the flies. Never told the men. They complained about the itching under the dressings but the maggots do the job very well. Debride the dead flesh. Clean the wounds. Never sleep. Never need breaks. Vigilant. Consistent. Persistent. Trustworthy. People aren't like that.'

Her face felt flushed and strange.

'Outside of perhaps dermatology, medicine generally isn't a good lifestyle for women. I wouldn't actually recommend women go to med school.'

She was flinching, her eye ticcing, and she controlled it.

'At least if they're married,' he said, 'there's some trust there. Some stability. Someone who ideally likes and supports the career. Children are a problem but not necessarily insurmountable. Do you think I'd be having this conversation if you were a man?'

'I've aborted one child for this job, Andrew, that was enough for me,' she said at last.

He sighed, and looked down at his desk.

'When I have a vested interest, Elizabeth, I act, irrespective of the risk.'

'I'm not sure what we're talking about here,' she said.

'Well, it's already decided.'

'What is decided.'

'You called me stupid, do you remember that? In the Morbidity and Mortality meeting you were quite rude to me.' He leaned back and half laughed.

'Is that what you're making this about?'

'I'm not making this about anything. This is what it is about. You might not ever have worked again, do you realise that? That *performance* in front of your colleagues. The quite public bisexual dalliances. The complaint from the family. Complaints from the nurses. Loco Liz, they call you. And now the embarrassing data.'

She openly sneered at him, and he laughed and then he stopped.

'I can honestly take you or leave you, Elizabeth,' he said.

'I see,' she said, and she nodded and nodded and sneered at him.

'No you don't,' he said. 'Because you're getting a second chance. You're back on call after a week's leave. It's already decided. If you fight this, none of it's going to go your way. There's to be a piece published in the *New Zealand Medical Journal*'s next issue on burnout and suicide and Richard's effects on your data. The spot's being held for us. You will contribute your name. We are going to control for the confounding of Richard, as it were. Young, inexperienced, out of his depth. He skewed the data. He was protected too much. You protected him too much. A lay media piece will follow in response to the boyfriend's very confused article discussing the recent patient death that was attributed to you. Front foot all the way. A tragedy for the hospital and the community that is now at an end with Richard's suicide. Staff counselling, a candlelight vigil, business as usual. I expect you there for it all. Faithful. Like a maggot, Elizabeth.'

'What is wrong with you,' she said.

'Now, how's that peer review coming along?' he said.

Their dates all end in 1986.

Sharon Christa McAuliffe, 1948–1986; Gregory Bruce Jarvis, 1944–1986; Judith Arlene Resnik, 1949–1986; Francis Richard 'Dick' Scobee, 1939–1986; Ronald Erwin McNair, 1950–1986; Michael John Smith, 1945–1986; Ellison Shoji Onizuka, 1946–1986.

The others carried on. Hardy, Ebeling, Nesbitt. Feynman. Boisjoly.

George Hardy, deputy director of science and engineering at Marshall Space Flight Center, argued with the Morton Thiokol engineers who warned of the mystery of the cold. They all got one line for which they became famous. Hardy's was: 'I am appalled. I am appalled by your recommendation.' Lawrence Mulloy, manager of the solid rocket booster programme, was supposed to have said: 'My God, Thiokol, when do you want me to launch, next April?' Thiokol vice-presidents overruled their engineers; they didn't have the data, they couldn't prove the danger. Mulloy and Hardy both took early retirement later in 86, and Mulloy was named in a US$15m negligence suit by an astronaut's wife. Their dates effectively end in 1986 too, though they carry on in quiet new worlds.

Nesbitt became famous for his commentary, the deadpan way he delivered his line: *Flight controllers here are looking very carefully at the situation. Obviously a major malfunction.* He was criticised for his tone. It caused another controversy when Beyoncé used the recording to open her song 'XO' in 2013. Nesbitt wasn't in fact rostered to report the launch that day. He'd volunteered for a colleague who was exhausted from staying up for delayed launch after delayed launch. After the accident Nesbitt was the last one to leave the empty offices of Mission Control and two years later volunteered to announce the first shuttle launch since *Challenger*. Because 'the last one ended badly'. For every launch thereafter, he told reporters, he would cross his fingers for the first two minutes and five seconds until the boosters separated. He was strange, like all the NASA men; dedicated and compassionate and strong, yet abstracted, and bad on camera. They got the tone wrong so many times.

Feynman became famous for putting a piece of twisted rubber in iced water live on TV during the Rogers Commission. Showing how slowly it returned to its previous shape. Making it all graspable. 'I believe this has some significance for our problem,' he said. A movie was made and he was played by William Hurt.

Ebeling, the Morton Thiokol engineer who warned Hardy about the cold, retired early after the accident. 'I couldn't stand another malfunction that I had anything to do with.' At Morton Thiokol he and Boisjoly and the others who testified were ostracised, became known as 'the five lepers'. After he retired Ebeling volunteered on a bird refuge and won an award for volunteer of the year. In 1990 he told a newspaper, 'Space is the new frontier. It's the future of things. Ducks are in the past tense.' He died in 2016, aged 89.

Boisjoly, who wrote a warning memo about cold O-rings in July 1985, died on January 6, 2012, of cancer of the colon, kidneys and liver. Boisjoly used the phrase 'away from goodness in the current database'. He sued Morton Thiokol twice, and became a speaker on workplace ethics, got depressed and had headaches. He reported being angry at his family, avoiding church. After he testified at the Commission the first woman in space, Sally Ride, hugged him. 'She was the only one,' a *New York Times* reporter wrote he 'whispered' to them in 1988. 'The only one.'

Whole careers go by with nothing else to compare; the mistakes like port-wine stains on their faces.

Something Vladi used to say. *Behind the data are people. Even if you do economic analysis, again, it's about people. And their souls are running around us, telling us: do it right.*

The doctors see them. Their ghosts in the passenger seats frowning back at them in traffic.

The recovered fragments of *Challenger* were analysed, coated with a grease preservative and buried underground in two disused missile siloes.

Two memories

She has two memories of her father that crowd out other memories now. She returns to them, especially when she's tired, and studies and revises them but they never change. They reify and increase in density. The sun and moon over the dissolving territory of her young adulthood. Her father gave her his old camera when she went to medical school. He was an amateur photographer and he had bought something digital. It was a Konica he'd used since he was a young man. She never used it at university and she lost it in one of the freezing flats she'd lived in in Dunedin. She never told him, never said anything to him. Afraid. When he died she found the camera boxed up with her stuff when she cleared out his house. The leather case filmed with grey mould. She'd forgotten that she'd taken it home and left it there and he'd had it the whole time, neither of them aware it was found, or, for him, that it was even lost.

167

Her father had good things. Ray-Ban Wayfarers from the 60s. A leather jacket. Good British boots he stopped wearing when the cartilage in his knees went. He cleaned the boots with his work shoes and her brown Rangi T-bars every Sunday night. Listening to National Radio. He warmed the nugget in a crude bain-marie on the stove. He had one rag for black and one rag for brown. The corners of the rags were stiff with old nugget till it softened under his hands. When he had his knees replaced he was taller by almost an inch. When the myocardial infarction killed him he was leaned against the hedge, watching her mow the small lawns of his new ownership flat. He fell as if in slow motion from that extra inch the surgery had gifted him, from that distance of the extra four years he walked without pain. The other memory is of the feeling of her father watching her work. That sea anchor dragging, the awful compromised feeling.

In the ICU

Wellington ICU was on the third floor. She walked there, up the stairs, beside her theatres, and she swiped her card at the main entrance. She saw Ben Matthews at the nurses' station on the ward. Black dress trousers and a blue gingham shirt. Dark short hair, dark eyes in Specsavers frames. Asymmetric face with a touch of eczema, half a sneer, half a neutral smile. Rubbing his hands together as he listened to two nurses in identical white polo shirts and blue trousers.

'Dr Matthews?' she said.

'Yup, that's me,' he said and assessed her.

'Hello.'

'Hello?' He laughed.

'Excuse us for a minute please,' Elizabeth said to the nurses.

He'd recognised her then and was looking at her differently. No more smile.

'Would you like us to take this somewhere,' he said.

'No, this is fine,' she said.

'What can I do for you. Elizabeth isn't it?'

'Taylor, that's right.'

'Pleased to meet you.'

'Pleased to meet you, too. I'd like to ask some questions

about a patient of ours.'

'Lisa Williams.'

'That's right.'

'What would you like to know?'

'I'd like to know about her time in ICU and how she died.'

He watched her face. He thought for a while, then he looked over towards the nurses in the station. They'd stopped talking.

'Are you sure you don't want a cup of coffee?' he said. 'We could head down to Wishbone, or an office?'

'No. This is fine.'

'Okay.'

'Okay.'

'Okay. All right. Lisa was transferred to us in ICU post-op, breathing spontaneously but with some difficulty. Low BP, tachycardic. We had her on a Hudson mask and my plan was for high-flow nasal oxygen and then try some CPAP if her sats dropped below 90. She was awake and oriented and she was tolerating a few sips of liquid. How much detail do you want, Mrs Taylor?'

'As much as you recall.'

'As much as I recall. Well, I might bring Jan in on this if you don't mind. Jan was running the ward.'

He looked over at the nurses and there were three and all of them were examining screens or notes.

'Jan? Can you help us out?'

They stood and looked at the nurses and the senior nurse in a purple shirt was signing some documents.

'So. The parents and the boyfriend were here for the death,' Matthews said.

'Uh huh.'

The senior nurse signed another document and said something and the other nurses laughed and then she turned towards them.

'I read that piece by the way and it was bullshit. That thing online they published,' he said before she was close enough to hear.

'It was his bullshit though. It was true for him.'

He watched her.

'Yes. Okay.'

The senior nurse had white hair and watchful eyes and her smile was stiff when she saw Elizabeth.

Matthews said, 'Jan, this is about Lisa Williams, 24-year-old girl. The sepsis from a little while ago now.'

'Oh.'

'Mrs Taylor here was her surgeon. Wants to know a bit about her admission.'

'Okay.'

'Okay,' Matthews said. 'We had her on the usual lines. We examined her surgical sites and they were clean. Her abdomen felt soft. She said she wasn't in pain and she was talking to the family. Awake, alert, talking in full sentences. Communicating her needs. Is this the sort of detail?'

'Yes, please,' Elizabeth said.

'They—were talking about a dog, a pet,' Matthews said.

'Uh huh. A dog?'

'And travel to the UK.'

'Uh huh.'

'In the next few hours Lisa said she had some head and neck pain that was eased temporarily by changing her position.'

'We changed her pillow, moved her around,' the senior nurse said beside her.

'Uh huh.'

'Her respiratory rate had increased. You tell it Jan.'

Jan looked Elizabeth in the eye. 'I sat with her from about

171

midnight. She was pretty high maintenance at this point.'

'What do you mean. I'd like details please.'

'I talked with her. About the UK and a trip she was going on. Because she didn't like the mask and she couldn't get comfortable.'

'Uh huh.'

'I had to keep explaining the importance of the mask. She was complaining that she was having to work harder and harder to breathe. The family had gone home at this point. The wee hours.'

'Uh huh.'

'At this juncture she was given midazolam for anxiety,' Matthews said. 'Sorry, Jan.'

'Um, so at about 3 a.m. she refused the CPAP mask and she had to be talked into it. She was clawing it off. We came up with a deal where we would keep the mask on for five minutes and she'd earn a sip of water.'

'Uh huh,' said Elizabeth. 'Go on.'

'By then,' said Matthews, 'she was deteriorating. The sepsis was advanced.'

'Uh huh.'

'She called out,' said the nurse.

'She was pale, anxious, agitated.'

'Uh huh.'

'She was dropping her sats. A breath about every two seconds. She was complaining of being tired and cold and the catheter was bothering her.'

'And the mask. She hated the mask.'

'Uh huh.'

'She was still speaking, just one to four word sentences and her breathing was very rapid and we called the registrar to see if she needed intubating. What time was that?'

'About three or four,' said Jan.

'So you were with her from midnight till four?' said Elizabeth to the nurse. 'Jan, is it?'

'Yes.'

'Okay.'

'I told her the doctor was coming and she was holding out for that.' The nurse's eyes were bright and wet. 'I wasn't there for the rest until the resuscitation.'

'The parents arrived about four,' Matthews said. 'We'd called them when we'd seen what was happening. We asked them to step outside as we were going to intubate her then put in a central line.'

'Uh huh.'

'We put her off to sleep. Ketamine and roc. Rocuronium. I can get Dr O'Connor in here if you'd like?'

'No, that's all right. What happened after that please?'

'I remember from Jim's notes he believes she arrested some time during induction and we began resuscitation at that point.'

'Uh huh.'

'We tried for about half an hour. I remember. She was just 24. Young, strong woman. Pronounced dead at four or five or something like that. The wee hours.'

'Thank you both,' said Elizabeth.

Matthews was watching her and the other nurse came up to stand beside Jan.

'I'm sorry about your colleague,' Matthews said.

'Thank you,' Elizabeth said.

'Is that . . . is that what you needed to know?'

'I think that's some of it,' she said. 'Very helpful, thank you.'

'Do you want more? Notes?'

'No, not from you. That's very helpful. Thank you. Thank you for . . . caring for my patient.'

He looked at her.

After a while Elizabeth said, 'The anaesthesia had not kicked in before the cardiac arrest, you think?'

'Jim didn't think so. No. I don't think so.'

'Was it at all lonely for her, at the end?' Elizabeth said.

Matthews looked at the nurse.

She blinked and looked at Elizabeth. 'We were all here,' she said. 'Her family were here right up until intubation. I was with her during the night.'

'You sat with her.'

'Yes.'

'About four hours, you said. Until the death at four. Or five.'

'Yes, I was here.'

'And your shift finished at midnight didn't it.'

The nurse shrugged.

'Okay,' said Elizabeth, and nodded at the linoleum. 'Thank you.'

'Okay?' said Matthews.

'Okay,' she said. 'Yes. Fine. Thank you all.'

Then she turned and left and they watched her go.

At 10 p.m. that night, 9 a.m. UK time, she called the *Royal London Journal of Medicine*.

'Denise Cohen?'

'Yes, hello Denise, this is Elizabeth Taylor.'

'Yes?'

174

'I'm an author of yours, working on the New Zealand editorial.'

'Oh of course yes, I'm sorry. First coffee of the day still pending, ha ha. Public reporting of surgical outcomes in New Zealand, now I'm with you.'

She was posh, multilevelled, like the editor in chief of the *Royal London* too.

'That's the one. Look, Denise, there have been some developments that affect the piece.'

'Oh?'

'Is there any time left for revisions?'

She was silent.

'Sorry,' Cohen said. 'I'm just at this moment staring across the desks of editorial towards where we keep our technical editors chained up like vicious dogs who are at present engaged in knocking your piece into shape. This goes to print tomorrow morning and will be live on the website tonight. Exactly what sort of revisions are we talking about?'

'I don't want to delay it. Here's the thing.'

She explained it as briefly and quickly as was possible. That 24 hours ago her registrar committed suicide after publication of the data. That there was currently in effect a cover-up going on. That his body was being thrown under the bus and that he was young and should have been supported and it should have been her that did it.

There was a lot to leave out. The elusiveness of a public record to do justice to the thrill of the work. The speed and light of it, and the stakes; competence. What it feels like to be good, how somehow abashing. The versions of the truth. The long tail of shame. Jessica screaming on the phone at her. *You killed my dog, you killed my dog.* Elizabeth saying, *I'm sorry, I'm so sorry.* Jessica screaming before she hung up,

175

You're an evil bitch and fucking psychopath. Jessica calling her back later that night to say, *I'm just really sad.* That they sat on the phone together in silence for five minutes. Meeting Robin for a lunch at Maranui and being unable to make eye contact after all this, and the café too crowded and the ambient noise too loud, too many echoes. Walking on the beach afterwards together, no wind and the skies the same pale steel as the sea. Robin saying, *I couldn't lie to them for you.* Elizabeth saying, *That's absolutely right.* Missing the movement of their hands together over a patient, how they used to dance. Missing work. Service. A covenant. *I will save you with my skills.* How lucky, actually, Robin was to survive this with a job. Because in the time of scandals nurses eat their young, and the surgeons help them feed. *Why don't you find the family*, Robin said gently. *Meet with them.* And not being able to answer that.

'Well, it's a faff, isn't it,' said Denise Cohen at last.

'Yep, well,' said Elizabeth.

'I'm sorry about your colleague.'

'Thank you.'

'Look, speaking from the perspective of the *Journal* which I'm bound to do, I can buy you a couple of hours. This warrants telling, but I *strongly* suggest you restrict yourself to two paragraphs, fore and aft, and we'll leave the edited body of the thing intact. The discussions about data strength, the *Lancet* paper, all good stuff. Leave it alone. That'll keep the tech eds reasonably happy. Tell us about Richard, the mistake, connect it with the data. You can make it personal, that's good, but not too personal. Can you do it in two paragraphs?'

'I can.'

'It's just an act of writing after all.'

'Just an act of writing,' Elizabeth said.

'Ha ha, yep. I know how it is. Now while you're here I can check some last minute things. Author affiliations. This is you and is it Andrew McGrath, capital M lower case c capital G, head of surgery, Wellington Hospital, etc etc. Have I got that right?'

'No, this is all me now.'

'All you?'

'Yep.'

'Right, fine, he's deleted. Two hours or it goes ahead with or without your additions.'

The two Bunnings employees stood back from the roller doors as the silver Camry came in fast first thing in the morning, bumping over the judder bars into the timberyard. The tyres squealed on the slick concrete inside as the big car went round the stacks of treated and untreated two by four and pulled up by the plasterboard.

The woman got out. They watched as she went to the stack and crouched and read the labels. One of the employees sighed and pulled the tape from his tape measure and let it flick back inside, and looked down at his poncho. The other one looked at him and sighed too.

'Fuck Tim, do a day's work.'

'Man, I'm just up.'

The boy walked over to the woman.

The Camry was classic period wagon, 2001 or 2 maybe, big 3-litre V6 and in good condition, not a single Wellington scratch. The back doors and the boot were open. There was a box in the back with two pails of Gib RediFilla and screws and tape and a pair of long ratchet straps.

'Gidday, can I help you?' the boy said.

'Nope,' she said to the stack, then, 'actually yes, this is it. Give us a hand.'

She dragged out two long slabs of the 2.4-metre gib plasterboard halfway and looked at him. He grabbed the other end and they lifted the heavy slabs off the stack.

'Dunno if you'll get these in the Camry,' the boy said, but she'd raised the boards head high and backed off and he had to follow her and then she circled round the back until they were holding the gib over the roof of the car between them.

'Stop there,' she said, 'and just lay it down.'

He did, and she swung it round straight.

'Um,' he said, 'look, sorry, we're not actually allowed to let you leave like that.'

She'd bent down and disappeared behind the car. The ratchet strap fell out of the passenger side door at his feet. He smiled and bent down and picked it up.

'Chuck it over,' she said. 'I won't tell anyone.'

He threw it over the top and she ratcheted the strap tight, tight enough to twang but not so it would crush the edges of the boards. He noted it. Then she tied the second one and then she went round the car closing the doors and paid in cash and drove out the timberyard doors with two and a half metres of gib plasterboard strapped on top of the roof of her car, illegally, slower now.

Acknowledgements

Thank you to the people who have blown and broadened my mind the last few years. Richard Hamblin is a constant inspiration to me—thank you for the graphs and analysis, but mostly for all you teach me. Thank you to Catherine Gerard, Maria Poynter, Jenny Hill, Nikolai Minko, Ying Li, Vince Carroll, Alexis Wevers, Lisa Hunkin, Natalie Horspool, Emily Mountier, Karen Jones, Jade Cincotta, Shelley Hanifan, Owen Ashwell, Di Sarfati, Iwona Stolarek, Gillian Bohm, Janice Wilson and Alan F. Merry—all of whom have given me an education in health, data and friendship.

Thank you to Ryan Skelton, always, for your constancy, your hunger and your faith. Thank you to my agent Imogen Pelham for believing in me and the work. Thank you to Ashleigh Young, Kirsten McDougall and Fergus Barrowman at VUP. Thanks to Damien Wilkins and Emily Perkins at the IIML for their support. Thank you to early readers Patrick Evans and Katy Robinson who nudged me gently in the right ways. Thanks to Cameron Law and Jeremy Hansen for good-humoured support and advice. Thank you to Sarah Mary Chadwick whose song 'Yunno What' gave me the entire sound of the book. Thank you Pip Adam for your inspiration and attitude.

Thank you to the clinicians of Wellington Regional Hospital. A book needs a setting and the actions described in this narrative do not reflect real people, practice, policy or particular cases at the current Wellington Hospital. We are lucky enough to have a public service that is full of dedicated and gifted individuals who care deeply for their profession and their patients. Some of these clinicians are named above. One of whom, Alex Psirides, was kind enough to give me some tips on getting complicated things right. Thank you. All errors of fact and description in this short book are my own.

To my first and best reader in every way, without whom I am lost: Anna Elisabeth Smaill, mother to my beloved son Alexander. And lastly to my daughter Lotte, who asks me what my book is about and always revives in me the fire and strange and simple urgency of that question: what happens?

CARL SHUKER is the author of five novels, including *Anti Lebanon*, *The Lazy Boys*, *Three Novellas for a Novel*, and *The Method Actors*, which won the 2006 Prize in Modern Letters. He is a former editor for *The British Medical Journal*, one of the oldest medical journals in the world, and principal publications adviser to the Health Quality & Safety Commission. He has lived and worked in Tokyo and London for many years, and now lives in his home country, New Zealand, with his wife and their two children.